PRIVATE ROYALS

JAMES PATTERSON is one of the best-known and biggest-selling writers of all time. His books have sold in excess of 300 million copies worldwide and he has been the most borrowed author in UK libraries for the past nine years in a row. He is the author of some of the most popular series of the past two decades – the Alex Cross, Women's Murder Club, Detective Michael Bennett and Private novels – and he has written many other number one bestsellers including romance novels and stand-alone thrillers.

James is passionate about encouraging children to read. Inspired by his own son who was a reluctant reader, he also writes a range of books for young readers including the Middle School, I Funny, Treasure Hunters, House of Robots, Confessions and Maximum Ride series. James is the proud sponsor of the World Book Day Award and has donated millions in grants to independent bookshops. He lives in Florida with his wife and son.

BOOK**SHOTS**

STORIES AT THE SPEED OF LIFE

What you are holding in your hands right now is no ordinary book, it's a BookShot.

BookShots are page-turning stories by James Patterson and other writers that can be read in one sitting.

Each and every one is fast-paced, 100% story-driven; a shot of pure entertainment guaranteed to satisfy.

Available as new, compact paperbacks, ebooks and audio, everywhere books are sold.

BookShots – the ultimate form of storytelling. From the ultimate storyteller.

PRIVATE ROYALS

JAMES
PATTERSON

WITH REES JONES

BOOK**SHOTS**

5 7 9 10 8 6 4

BookShots
20 Vauxhall Bridge Road
London SW1V 2SA

BookShots is part of the Penguin Random House
group of companies whose addresses can be found at
global.penguinrandomhouse.com

 Penguin
Random House
UK

First published by BookShots in 2016

www.penguin.co.uk

A CIP catalogue record for this book is available
from the British Library

ISBN 9781786530172

Typeset in Garamond Premier Pro font 11/15.5 pt in
India by Thomson Digital Pvt Ltd, Noida Delhi

Printed and bound in Great Britain by Clays Ltd, St Ives Plc

MIX
Paper from
responsible sources
FSC® C018179

Penguin Random House is committed to a sustainable future
for our business, our readers and our planet. This book is made
from Forest Stewardship Council® certified paper.

PROLOGUE

HE HATED HER.

He hated her high cheekbones. He hated her perfect smile. He hated the way her auburn hair cascaded over her shoulders like a Rocky Mountain waterfall. He hated her painted fingernails that had never known dirt. He hated her ill-deserved confidence, wealth and station. He hated her class and what it said about his country, but most of all, he hated her because she was throwing it all away.

It was enough hate to make him want to kill her.

But not yet. Maybe never, if the price was right. For now he would watch. He would weigh his decisions. He had to think, because the stuck-up bitch had given him one more reason to hate her.

She had changed her plans. Plans that he had studied. Plans that he'd assessed. Plans that he'd used as the blueprint for his own concept of operations.

No plan survived contact with the enemy, he knew that, and this pouting loudmouth was his enemy now. A lesser enemy than he had ever faced, but the stakes were higher. So much higher.

And the moment was drawing near.

He watched from behind the living room door, opened just a crack, as she chopped the cocaine into lines on a silver plate, using a metallic business card that she kept for the purpose, and snorted it through a cut-down drinking straw taken from the kitchen of her Chelsea apartment. This was no casual Friday evening, but the streamlined consumption of an addict.

And what of that stick-thin apparition beside her? The tabloids and gossip magazines called her an 'It Girl'. To the watching man, she was a coked-up distraction – an enabler – and one that should have been on the other side of London.

Still, addicts were not known for their adherence to schedules, and the man had planned for distractions. In every crisis lay opportunity, and this 'It Girl' could prove either valuable or useful. When trying to make a point of your deadly intent, it never hurt to have an extra head that you could cut from its shoulders. The man smiled sickly as he pictured his blade against her pencil-thin neck. For a moment, he wondered if her red eyes were even capable of expressing fear, then snapped himself from his daydream.

Yes, the It Girl would provide an opportunity, if only one for pleasure. But for now he cast his eyes back to his primary target, pleased to see that the ketamine he had cut into her coke was taking effect, the horse tranquilliser bringing the pair down from the rapid dialogue of their powdered high and leaving them slumped heavily on a ten-thousand-pound sofa that was stained with red wine.

It was time.

The man stood. He pushed open the door.

Her head turned slowly towards the movement. There was no hate or anger in her eyes, only drug-fuelled confusion, and he wondered if she could see the malice in his.

He put a finger to her plush lips. The beautiful girl nodded her understanding, as docile as a puppy as he pulled the knife from his pocket.

A moment later the blood began to pour.

CHAPTER 1

AS A FORMER US Marine, an avid traveller, and now head of the world's foremost investigation agency, Jack Morgan had set foot in some of the most grandiose buildings on the planet, and yet he was always taken aback by the majesty of London's iconic architecture.

'Do you know that Horse Guards Parade was first built in 1664?' he asked the man beside him.

'I didn't,' replied Peter Knight, the wiry Englishman who was the head of Private's London office. 'That's over a hundred years older than your country, isn't it?' He smiled and prodded his friend and boss.

'I'd give you a lesson in history now,' Morgan replied, 'but I'm a little outnumbered here.'

Knight laughed as he took in their surroundings. Dozens of British servicemen and women milled beneath the awnings erected at the edge of Horse Guards Parade, but it was champagne flutes that complemented their ceremonial uniforms, not rifles and bayonets.

'Just don't get nervous tomorrow when you see the redcoats.' Knight grinned.

Both he and Morgan wore light summer suits, the June weekend shaping up to be hot and muggy. As a former serviceman himself, Morgan spared a thought for the soldiers who would be standing to attention for hours during the next day's Trooping the Colour parade.

'Glad it's not going to be you on that parade square?' Knight asked, reading his friend's thoughts.

'I'm happier taking in the view, and having this in my hand.' Morgan smiled, holding up his drink. 'I'd be happier still if we were here to secure these events, rather than watching from the sidelines.'

Private had been among a raft of security providers who'd bid for the lucrative contracts to oversee the major events for the Queen's ninetieth birthday celebrations. To Morgan's displeasure, and Knight's embarrassment, Private had not landed a single one.

'It's not on you, Peter,' Morgan told his friend, seeing the slightest of slumps in the Englishman's shoulders. 'This is the old boys' club, and the right school or regiment means more sometimes than service and price.'

Knight nodded his understanding. As a former special investigator to the Old Bailey, he had seen first-hand how Britain's aristocratic class system could still hold sway.

'That's all well and good, Jack, but I don't want people to get hurt because we didn't know a secret handshake.'

'Well, we're here,' Morgan declared brightly, 'so let's enjoy the champagne.'

'Cheers,' Knight offered as the men touched glasses.

'Enjoying the drinks, gentlemen?' they were asked in the nasal tone of the British gentry.

'Colonel De Villiers,' Morgan greeted the Coldstream Guards officer.

At six foot three, Colonel Marcus De Villiers, head of security for the royal family's inner circle, made for an imposing man. He was also the reason why Private had no hand in the security for the Queen's birthday events.

'I'm surprised to see you here, Mr Morgan.' The Colonel's words were neutral, but his eyes betrayed his irritation.

'We were invited,' Knight answered for them.

'Oh.'

Morgan smiled, imagining how the Colonel would be kicking himself inwardly for not having scrutinised the guest list more closely.

A proud man with little time for cocky Americans, De Villiers sneered as he looked at the men's champagne flutes.

'I imagine you made full use of the hospitality provided at the Olympic Games, also? Little wonder that Cronus and his Furies did such damage.' The Colonel was referring to the bloodthirsty murderers who had run amok during the 2012 London Olympics, before finally being brought down by the two men who held their tongues, refusing to take the bait. 'I suppose you did catch him at the closing ceremony, at least.' De Villiers shrugged.

'Peter did, yes, Colonel,' Morgan replied. 'He put his life at risk to save others.' He eyed the thin row of medals on the Colonel's chest and saw none that would signify combat. 'As a military man, I'm sure you would understand all about courage and sacrifice.'

De Villiers was stung by the sarcasm. 'Private investigators should stick to photographing unfaithful spouses, *Mr* Morgan. Good evening.'

The Colonel turned on his heel, and Knight couldn't help but smirk. 'Sounds like someone's made use of that service,' he said.

Morgan laughed and ran a hand through his hair to clear himself of the irritation De Villiers had caused him. As he did so, the American locked eyes with the most beautiful woman present amongst the crowd of cocktail dresses and uniforms.

And she came straight for him.

CHAPTER 2

MORGAN WATCHED AS THE beauty closed the space between them, never once breaking eye contact, confidence radiating from her in waves. Morgan made for a striking figure himself, and was no stranger to women finding him attractive, but even he was a little shocked by the brazen approach that had come from nothing but a look.

'Jane Cook,' the beautiful woman introduced herself, putting out her hand.

Morgan had seen a lot of stunning women in his time, but he didn't know if he'd seen any so attractive when wearing the drab green uniform of the military, and with no make-up.

'Jack Morgan.' He smiled, taking her hand, and quickly ran his eyes over the insignia and decorations of her uniform – she was *Major* Jane Cook of the Royal Horse Artillery, a veteran of Afghanistan and Iraq, and recipient of an OBE.

'I know who you are, Mr Morgan,' she told him. 'I invited you.'

'Jane is a friend of mine,' Knight announced. 'I need to check in with the office. Back in a tick.'

'That's very nice of Peter,' she smiled as Knight took his leave, 'but I'd also like to think of myself as a candidate. I leave the service at the end of the year, Mr Morgan, and I'd like you to be my next employer.'

Realising that the attention towards him was due to business and not pleasure, Morgan almost laughed aloud at his own ego.

'Peter will take care of you, Major, and we'll see if you're the right fit for Private. I'm afraid I'm only here to watch a show. My company has no stake in the celebrations.'

'De Villiers,' Cook said, casting an icy glance towards the man. 'The closest he ever came to combat was an air-conditioned office in Bahrain. I'm sorry you were screwed by him on the contracts, Mr Morgan. I can tell you from personal experience that I know what an institutionalised old boys' club the British security forces can be.'

'Call me Jack. And it is what it is. Believe me, there are cliques and fraternities in the American hierarchy too.'

'So what brings you here to London, if not work?' she asked.

'Heading back from Europe across the pond, so I wanted to see how my guys are getting along here. I've always wanted to see the Trooping the Colour parade, so when Peter told me that he had invitations, I could hardly refuse.'

'Well, I'm glad you'll get to experience something new here in London.' Cook's eyes gave the slightest suggestion that marching soldiers were not all the city had to offer. 'Home is LA?'

'The Palisades. It's the bit between LA and Malibu.'

'Malibu? Do you surf?'

'It's the second-best way I know to clear my head.' Morgan smiled.

Cook fought a losing battle to stop herself from doing the same. 'I surf. In Cornwall,' she managed, on the edge of blushing.

Morgan said nothing. His own smile was gone.

Because Knight was on his way back in a hurry, and Morgan recognised the look on his friend's face.

'They need us at headquarters,' Knight informed his boss. 'Now.'

CHAPTER 3

WITH MORGAN ON HIS shoulder, Knight pushed open the door to his office in Private London's headquarters.

Neither of them were surprised to see the grey-haired gentleman inside.

He stood at the window, looking out over the city, his hands clasped behind a bespoke tailored suit. His outward appearance suggested calm and confidence, even when standing alone inside a stranger's office. It was an appearance that would fool almost anybody.

But Jack Morgan and Peter Knight were not just anybody, and they could see the tension in the man's posture and hear his exaggerated breathing.

They knew who he was, of course – no one could waltz into Private, let alone Knight's office, without the say-so of someone in a position of authority. Knight had granted his because his workspace was sterile, all files deeply encoded on drives that were unobtainable unless the man at the window had been a master hacker.

And he was not. He was the ageing Duke of Aldershot, and a member of the royal family.

'Sir,' Knight said simply, and the man turned towards them.

On the journey from Horse Guards, a quick Internet search had revealed the Duke to be sixty years old. However, with his red eyes and pale skin, the royal looked closer to a hundred.

'Please, sir, take a seat,' Knight offered, worried that the man was moments from collapse. Without a word, the Duke complied.

Morgan hung back by the door as Knight poured the Duke a glass of water and pulled his own chair forward so that he was at arm's length from him.

'I can get tea or coffee if you like, sir?' Knight asked. The Duke shook his head and the water remained untouched, trembling in his hands.

'Your Grace,' Knight began, patiently, 'we know who you are, and whatever the problem is, we can help you with it. Why are you here?'

The Duke's haunted eyes showed the first signs of life.

'Abbie,' he mumbled.

'Your daughter?' Knight asked, recognising her name from his Internet search on the Duke. 'Is she in trouble?'

The Duke nodded slowly, a pair of tears racing down his pale cheeks. 'Yes,' he gasped.

'How do you know, sir?' Morgan asked from the doorway.

The Duke's eyes widened as he turned towards the American's voice.

'I will show you.'

CHAPTER 4

CHANGED INTO HIS STREET clothing of jeans and a roll-sleeved shirt, Knight pulled the Range Rover to a stop at Chelsea Harbour, the Duke and a hoody-wearing Morgan emerging from its back seat. The ride had been quiet, the investigators wanting to hold their questions for the Duke until they had set eyes on what he assured them was the scene of a crime.

'Nice place,' Morgan said quietly to Knight, casting his eyes across the rows of moored boats. 'He says hers is the centre penthouse.' He pointed at a block of luxury apartments.

'Wonder what the rent is on that,' Knight said.

'About seven million to buy.'

Knight was about to ask Morgan how he knew, but the confident smile of the handsome man told him the full story.

'Leave some for the rest of us, will you?' Knight grinned, turning to see a white transit van pull up behind the Range Rover.

'The cavalry has arrived,' the van's driver announced from its window in an east London accent.

'Good to see you, Hooligan.' Morgan smiled, extending his hand to the man who was the guru when it came to all things forensic, scientific and technological at Private London.

'Good to see you too, Jack.'

'Your Grace, this is Jeremy Crawford,' Knight introduced the scruffy man more formally.

'Call me Hooligan, Duke' he insisted. Red-haired and freckled, the self-confessed geek had earned the nickname for his love of all things West Ham, and wore the moniker as a badge of honour.

The Duke said nothing, and seemed to shrink at the sight of the building in front of them.

'It's OK, sir. The sooner you take us inside, the sooner we can make sure your daughter's safe.'

Morgan wanted to reassure the Duke. But once they'd entered the building and gone into the penthouse apartment, he feared he may have spoken too soon.

The room was awash with blood.

'Bloody 'ell,' Hooligan exclaimed before catching himself. 'I'll get to work on some samples then, shall I?'

'Do it,' Morgan agreed, then turned to Knight. 'Peter. Elaine still at Scotland Yard?' Elaine was the sister of Knight's deceased wife, and was a well-respected inspector on London's Metropolitan Police Force.

'Want me to call it in?'

'No police!' the Duke said urgently, coming alive. 'He'll kill her!' He pointed a shaking finger at the kitchen countertop.

Morgan stepped carefully to it, and cast his eyes over the granite.

A message had been scrawled in blood:

'I HAVE YOUR DAUGHTER.'

CHAPTER 5

MORGAN AND KNIGHT STEPPED out onto the balcony that overlooked the rows of moored boats beneath them, millions of pounds' worth of pleasure craft sitting gently on the water.

'He's right about the police,' Morgan sighed, leaning against the railing. 'We bring them in, Abbie's chances of making it out alive go down big time.'

'Maybe,' Knight mused. 'But this isn't Mexico, Jack. Nobody's going to tip off the kidnappers.'

'It's not our call to make, Pete.'

'This doesn't hit me as a normal kidnapping though.' Knight shook his head. 'A royal gets taken the night before Trooping the Colour? Seems like more than a coincidence. But why not take a royal who's more prominent? Abbie's pretty distant to the throne.'

'Did you see some of those photos inside?' Morgan asked. Abbie's apartment was full of frames of her on the arms of A-list celebrities. 'She's had the media attention to make her as known to the public as the inner circle of the royal family, but she only has a fraction of the security. Her dad says she has one bodyguard, and he's not even with her twenty-four–seven.'

'Kidnapping a royal the easy way,' Knight summed up.

The pair lapsed into silence, minds churning over the reasons why Abbie Winchester would be the target of a kidnap, and the solutions to retrieve her safely.

'The Duke was explicit that he didn't want the police involved,' Knight thought aloud, 'but Trooping the Colour is the army's baby. We can keep them in the loop, in case this is all connected, without breaking our contract to him.'

'A liaison.' Morgan nodded, liking the idea, and then smiling as the candidate for the position became clear. 'You know who I'm thinking of, don't you?'

Knight did. He flicked through the contacts in his phone and handed it over to Jack. 'She can be the army's eyes and ears, but if she wants to come work for us, then we don't need to worry about her stepping on our toes.'

Morgan nodded in agreement as he dialled the number and spoke into the phone. 'This is Jack Morgan. Are you ready for your assessment?'

CHAPTER 6

THE DUKE SAT ALONE in the Range Rover's back seat, gazing through the window at nothing. Up front, Morgan powered up a tablet as Knight drove them back across the city to Private HQ.

'The office has sent us the packet on Abbie,' Morgan said quietly to Knight. This was the initial dossier Private staff had compiled on the victim. A quick glance at the content told Morgan it was best he share the rest with Knight when they were not in the presence of the girl's father, and so he read on in silence.

Twenty-five-year-old Abbie Winchester was cousin to the popular future king of the United Kingdom, and had once been the model royal, heavily involved in charity work the world over. Then, three years ago, Abbie's mother had died from breast cancer, and the daughter had quickly slid into the role of the party girl, pictured blitzed drunk from St Tropez to Dubai. The tabloids loved her in the way that they loved all train wrecks, and Abbie soon became synonymous with excess and hedonism, leaving a trail of rock- and sports-star lovers in her wake.

Naturally, the charities with which Abbie had done so much good work had ditched her quickly to avoid tarnishing their own images. The royal family had been more discreet in their handling of matters but, slowly and surely, they had distanced themselves from the wayward young woman.

Morgan asked the Duke if he and his family had been invited to the Trooping the Colour ceremony.

'Yes,' the Duke replied, turning to face him, his distraught mind still sharp enough to read the unspoken question in the American's eyes. 'They can't keep us away from everything. That's why I had gone to her apartment, to see that she was all ready for the morning.'

'You said she had a bodyguard, sir?' Morgan asked.

'Bodyguard and chaperone. He was supposed to be there tonight, to keep an eye on her. He's been off a lot recently, some kind of virus that left him ghastly and weak, but he called my secretary this evening to check in, and to confirm that he would be with her.'

'Who is he?'

'Aaron Shaw. He served under me as troop sergeant. Household Cavalry.'

'You were in the army?' Morgan asked.

'It's expected. In my bloodline,' the Duke answered with a shrug, finding some focus with the distraction of conversation. 'Shaw's a fine man. Never let me down, not once. He'd die for my family.'

Morgan managed a weak smile. 'I hope it won't come to that, sir,' he told the Duke.

But remembering the amount of blood in the apartment, Jack knew that may have happened already.

CHAPTER 7

ABBIE OPENED HER EYES.

She knew instantly that she was on a comedown. Her skull felt as if it were packed with candyfloss; her lips were dry and cracked. She pushed herself up on her elbows, hoping she might find some kind of fruit juice and vodka to take away the edge – her usual comedown cure.

Instead, she found herself somewhere she didn't recognise.

There were four walls, but no windows or doors. The walls, ceiling and floor all seemed to be covered in the same swirling pattern. Abbie laughed, happy that she must still be tripping. The comedown could wait.

She looked more closely at the content of her lucid dream. She was on a single bed with a thin mattress. It was the only furniture in the room, but on the floor was a collection of bottles, a tray of sandwiches and a silver plate. Abbie moved towards it and was glad to see that it was loaded with powder. She took a noseful, and the tang of it hit her in the back of the throat. She sank back onto the bed and noticed a black object on the swirling ceiling.

As she drifted into the comfort of the ketamine, she had no idea that the black object was a camera.

CHAPTER 8

HAVING LEFT THE DUKE at his central London residence under the watch of two Private employees, Knight pulled the Range Rover to a stop outside Private HQ. No sooner had they climbed out than Jane Cook appeared from within and strode purposefully towards them.

'I'm ready,' she told Morgan.

'You're not,' he answered with a smile, taking in Cook's trouser suit.

'Why?' she asked, and Morgan paused before answering – Cook looked fantastic, but he brought his mind back to the task at hand.

'You look like a cop,' he told her, then pointed to his own outfit of jeans and a dark hooded jacket.

'Pays to not stand out,' Knight added, knowing that Cook would turn heads regardless of what she wore.

'I'll go change,' she said.

'No time,' Morgan said, taking the keys from Knight. 'You're coming with me.'

'OK. Where to?'

'There was a bodyguard with Abbie, so we're going to check out his place. We can find you a new wardrobe as and when,' Morgan explained, then tossed her the Range Rover's keys. 'And you're driving.'

With Morgan and Cook heading out into the relative calm of London's Friday-night traffic, Knight waited for Hooligan to arrive in the van. Sensing that the night would be a long one, he made use of the moment of peace to call his children's babysitter, who had luckily been booked to cover Knight for his cocktail evening with Morgan.

'Been talkin' to the little 'uns?' Hooligan asked a few minutes later as he climbed from the transit van. 'Always got a big grin on ya mug when ya do.'

'When you have kids, you'll understand, mate,' Knight laughed.

The scruffy geek shook his head, affronted by the idea. 'Can't tie this body down to one bird, son. Be a crime.'

'You're a real giver, Hooligan.'

The men carried the boxes of evidence inside the building and into Hooligan's state-of-the-art lab.

'How long will it take to come back with results from the blood samples we took from the scene?' Knight asked.

'Could be an hour, could be never.' Hooligan shrugged. 'The Duke gave me a sample of his royal DNA, so if it's his daughter, then we should know pretty sharpish.'

'And the bodyguard? He seems like the most likely donor.'

'He ex-military? See if your liaison can pull some strings and get his records. Either that or something with DNA from his place.'

'The military keep DNA records?' Knight asked.

'Identifying body parts,' Hooligan explained.

Knight promised he would do what he could, and left the London native to work his magic. Until the kidnappers called there was little Knight could do but try to build up as detailed a picture as possible of Abbie's life. To that end, he invited a guest into the office.

'Sadie Wilkinson,' announced a hawk-faced woman in her mid-thirties as she walked into Private's secure reception area.

'Peter Knight.'

'I know exactly who you are, Mr Knight. I watched the footage of you taking down Cronus at the Olympics closing ceremony.'

'Oh.'

'You know, with me and the right agent, we could have made you rich.'

'Unfortunately, Mrs Wilkinson—'

'Miss.'

'*Miss* Wilkinson. Unfortunately, I didn't ask you in at this hour for my own benefit. I asked you because you're Abbie Winchester's publicist.'

'That you did, and I must say I'm intrigued. So, why am I here?'

'Abbie's been kidnapped,' Knight told her straight, instantly regretting his blunt approach – because Miss Wilkinson fell into his arms.

CHAPTER 9

AS THE RANGE ROVER crossed Tower Bridge to the southern bank of the Thames, Morgan's phone began to vibrate.

'HQ,' he told Cook, then answered the call through the car's Bluetooth connection.

'Boss, it's Hooligan. Got an unknown number calling the Duke's line now. I'm patching you.'

Morgan looked over at Cook behind the wheel. There was no sign of apprehension there, her eyes on the traffic, hands resting lightly on the controls.

'Hello?' said the Duke, his voice edged with fear. The voice that answered him was cold and metallic – the kidnapper was using a filter.

'Let's keep this very simple, Duke. I have your daughter, and if you don't want to see her head thrown in front of the cameras at Trooping the Colour, then I want thirty million by eleven a.m. tomorrow morning.'

'Thirty million?' the Duke gasped.

'Or her head goes bouncing in front of the cameras, and everyone around the world will get to see it. Understand?'

'I understand.' The Duke paused a moment. 'What about her bodyguard? What have you done with him?' Morgan nodded in approval – he had instructed the Private men on the scene to ensure the Duke asked that question.

'Operators aren't my concern,' the cold voice uttered. 'Spoilt little daughters are. Eleven hundred hours, thirty million in notes, or her head.'

The line went dead.

'Take us off conference,' Morgan instructed. 'Hooligan, you still with me?'

'Yeah, just you and me, boss.'

'Send me a recording of the call, will you?'

'I'll do it now.'

'What did you get from that?' Morgan asked Cook as he hung up the call and waited for the recording.

'The kidnapper used "I",' Cook answered. 'I think we're dealing with one man.'

'Why a man?'

'Even with the filter on the voice, there was no way that was a woman.'

Morgan nodded his agreement. Moments later Hooligan delivered the recording of the call. Morgan opened the audio file and listened to the kidnapper's chilling words over and over.

'Something wrong?' Cook asked, seeing Morgan's eyes narrow and his shoulders tighten.

'Change of plan,' he told her, confirming that something *was* wrong. 'We're not going to the bodyguard's place. I'll have Peter send one of his guys there instead.'

'OK. So where to for us?'

'Horse Guards.'

CHAPTER 10

KNIGHT PUSHED OPEN THE door to Hooligan's lab. 'What did I miss?'

'Oh, only the kidnapper calling. Where have you been?'

'Don't ask.' Knight shook his head.

But the East Ender asked again anyway.

'Abbie's publicist came in to help me build background on her,' said Knight. 'She'd know the darker parts of Abbie's life that her father wouldn't.'

'She would?'

'Half of a publicist's job is covering things up, or at least glossing them over,' Knight explained.

'Did she help?'

'Not really. She fainted into my arms.'

Hooligan smiled. 'You're getting as bad as the boss.'

Knight ignored the comment. 'What have we got on the bloods?'

'Bad news for the bodyguard. Looks like the bulk of the blood is his. Matched his military records that Cook got for us. There must have been six or seven pints of it.'

'He'd never survive that.'

'Nope. I'm afraid the bodyguard's brown bread.'

'Anything turn up at his place?' asked Knight.

'Seemed to live a sanitary life. Some dirty gym clothes in the wash basket. No computer equipment that we could take a sneaky look at.'

'What else have you got?'

'A few strands of cotton in the blood pool,' said Hooligan. 'Look like they were cut with a serrated edge. Most likely a hunting knife.'

Knight looked at the slides Hooligan projected onto the wall, seeing the frayed fibres.

'That much blood, the blade must have severed an artery.'

'That's what I thought,' Hooligan agreed. 'But there was no arterial spray in the penthouse. A wound like that's usually a wild hosepipe.'

'Armpit?' Knight suggested, remembering cases he'd seen from his time at the Old Bailey. 'Stand up,' he instructed Hooligan. 'Now, say I'm coming at you with a blade and I go for your chest. What's your natural instinct?'

'I lift my arm to protect myself,' Hooligan answered.

'Exactly, and my blade goes into your armpit and hits the subclavian artery. Then, your natural reaction will be to bring your arm back down again, covering the wound and causing the blood to pool on the floor, rather than spurt all over the walls and furniture.'

'That makes sense,' Hooligan admitted.

'You said the bulk of the blood is from the bodyguard,' Knight said.

'There was a second set of markers in one of my samples. Definitely from a different person,' Hooligan explained.

'Who?'

'A female, and cross-checking it against her father's sample, it's not Abbie. Have we got a female kidnapper?'

Knight shook his head. 'I think we've got a second hostage.'

CHAPTER 11

JACK MORGAN STOOD ALONE on the Victoria Embankment of the River Thames. He was beneath the Royal Air Force memorial, the gilded eagle glinting in the sun as the last light of the balmy June evening finally died. The London Eye twinkled on the opposite bank.

'Mr Morgan.' Colonel De Villiers greeted him with the minimum courtesy his aristocratic upbringing would allow. 'I trust you have a good reason to interrupt my preparations for tomorrow's parade.'

'The best reason, Colonel,' Morgan replied, remaining civil for the sake of Abbie. 'To save lives.'

'Major Cook said as much on the phone, which is why I'm here.'

'And I appreciate your time.'

'I find most Americans to be direct, Mr Morgan. Would you be so good as to tell me what this is about?'

Morgan was happy to oblige, his manner calm. 'Abbie Winchester has been kidnapped, and will be killed during tomorrow's parade if a ransom is not paid.'

'According to whom?' De Villiers asked, dismissively.

'Her kidnapper.'

'Who is?'

'We're working on that,' Morgan answered, holding the Colonel's disdainful stare.

'By "we", I imagine you mean Private, otherwise I would be having this conversation with the police, as would be proper. However, I suppose it is the Duke's money to throw away as he likes.'

'Who you are talking to isn't the important part, Colonel.' Morgan spoke evenly, restraining the urge to shake the sneer from the man's empty skull.

De Villiers smiled and looked out over the Thames as he answered, perhaps wishing he could throw the American into its waters. 'Mr Morgan, I have worked closely with the royal family for the past two years. Abbie Winchester is a drunken slut and an embarrassment. No doubt this whole ploy is some kind of attention-grabbing exercise of hers to get into the tabloids. I shan't be a party to it.'

'There was blood at the scene, Colonel,' Morgan revealed. 'Enough to suggest the person it came from is dead.'

He expected the revelation to hit home, hard. Instead, De Villiers merely shrugged.

'Then perhaps she finally pissed off the wrong drug dealer or fucked the wrong brain-dead rock star,' said the Colonel. 'I don't pretend to know what goes on inside that girl's head, Mr Morgan, but I do know that it is no concern of mine – the security of the inner circle of the royal family is, and my focus is on tomorrow's parade. Good evening, Mr Morgan. I have a final planning meeting to attend.'

'You may want to revisit those plans, Colonel,' Morgan told him, his patience at an end and his tone hardening.

'Oh really, Mr Morgan? And why is that?'

Morgan thought of holding back the information, but the life of Abbie Winchester had to come before his dislike of De Villiers, and so he told the officer the reason why. 'Because the man whose blood it is was from your own ranks.'

CHAPTER 12

REJOINING COOK IN THE Range Rover, Morgan instructed the soldier to follow the Thames along its northern bank. 'Head towards the Tower of London.'

On the way, Cook asked, 'You think this is all a smokescreen for a heist?' referring to the precious Crown jewels held within the Tower's walls.

Morgan shook his head. 'No, but I like your lateral thinking. We're going to see an acquaintance of mine. An ex-SAS guy known as Flex. Falklands and Desert Storm vet. You know him?'

'Those guys stick to themselves.'

As they neared the Tower of London, Morgan told her, 'Flex runs a private security firm now.' He pointed Cook in the direction she should drive.

'So he's your business rival?'

'Not really. Cases like Abbie, people come to Private. If someone wants mercenaries for Africa, or an escort into Syria, they go to Flex.'

'And it's all above board?'

'You tell me.' Morgan smiled, eyeing the half-dozen Bentleys and Aston Martins in the security firm's underground garage.

'He buys British, at least,' Cook offered as they walked towards reception. 'Won't he be back at home at this time?' she asked, glancing at her watch. It was coming up to midnight.

'He lives here. Hates to commute, and he has people in every time zone.'

'Why would someone want to live in their office?'

'You'll see.'

And after a thorough security check, and a twenty-storey ride in a lift, Cook did. The office's view was breathtaking: the building looked out over the iconic features of Tower Bridge, HMS *Belfast* and the Shard on the opposite side of the Thames.

The sight of Michael 'Flex' Gibbon was almost as impressive. Standing at five foot eight, Flex was a fifty-year-old muscle-bound mass who looked as if he'd been carved from granite.

'Jack!' he said, taking Morgan's hand in his vice-like grip. 'Who's this?' he asked, looking at Cook.

'Good to see you, Flex,' said Morgan. 'This is Major Jane Cook.'

'Major?' Flex asked, surprised. 'You look more like a cop,' he told her, taking in the trouser suit and causing Morgan to break into an 'I told you so' smile.

'So, I imagine it's business at this hour?' the big man said.

'It is.' Morgan nodded. 'Hope we didn't wake you up.'

'Not at all, mate. Just got off the phone to Nairobi. All going to shit down there – again. I took the kids on holiday there once. Can you believe that? Now look at it. Bloody savages, all of them, but they keep a man in business.'

'Business is good?'

Flex shrugged his mountainous shoulders. 'The glory days have gone, mate. Too many companies now, and too many ex-soldiers with war in their heads who can't settle into working a civvie job. Everyone's undercutting everyone. Times are tight, so I hope you're not here for a loan.'

Morgan laughed. 'It's a personnel matter, actually.'

'Oh? I'd be happy to subcontract guys to you, Jack. You know I only take on the best.'

Morgan shook his head. 'I'm working a kidnapping,' he explained, 'and something the kidnapper said has me thinking he may have crossed your path at some point.'

'Go on?'

'He used the word "operator" in the ransom call to describe the bodyguard. That's a term only someone in our circles would use.'

Flex nodded in agreement. 'Private military contractors are usually known as operators, yeah, but still, I don't see how that can really help you, Jack. There's hundreds of thousands of guys working this kind of gig now, from all over the world.'

'But how many of them crossed paths with our victim's bodyguard?'

'Why don't you ask him?' Flex said, puzzled.

'He's dead.'

'Oh.' Flex was no stranger to death. 'He won't be much use then.'

'His name was Aaron Shaw, and it looks as if the killer was able to get close to him. There were no signs of forced entry at the site, so we're working on the theory that he was probably a friend, or at least trusted. We need to know more about Shaw. Did he have a clique? Regular work partners?'

'One moment,' Flex told them and left the room.

Cook joined Morgan at the window in silence, the pair enjoying the tranquillity of the city's glittering lights.

'Aaron Shaw,' Flex announced on his way back in, tossing the file in his hand onto the spacious desk. 'He applied to work for me two years ago, but you're shit out of luck I'm afraid, Jack.'

'And why's that?'

'Shaw was in the Household Cavalry Regiment, and I only take on ex-infantry or special forces. I don't trust a soldier who doesn't want to look his enemy in the eye when he kills him.'

'I was a helicopter pilot.'

'I know.' The big man grinned. 'But I like you anyway, Jack, so I'll make some calls.'

CHAPTER 13

ABBIE OPENED HER EYES. She looked around her, and she wanted to cry.

The plate was empty. The powder was gone.

She ran her finger across the metal, hoping a few remaining grains might stick to her skin. She rubbed what little there was into her gums. They numbed, slightly, but it did little to take the edge off her anxiety – the fear of the inevitable crash after the highs, and the crushing realisation that she was not in her home.

Nor in anyone's home, as far as she could tell.

Abbie looked at the four walls around her, hating the way the swirling patterns made her vision swim. She looked at the bed, and for the first time noted that it was bolted to the floor. Then she saw the lonely bucket in the corner of the small room, and the black object above her on the ceiling.

It was a camera, she realised.

Why the hell was there a camera on the ceiling?

Her heart beat faster, the pounding of blood in her temples at first obscuring the sounds from beyond the walls, but then she was sure of it. It reminded her of the mice in the family's country manor house, scratching and scuffling out of sight – but this was too big to be any rodent.

And then Abbie heard the voices. Not words. Only voices. They were commanding. They were angry. Someone was arguing, and amongst that chaos there was the plaintive pleading of a person struck by the most terrible fear.

She stumbled to her feet, putting her ear to the cold metal wall. 'Who's out there?' she shouted.

'Abbie?' someone sobbed. And then came a scream.

The kind of scream that marks the end of a life.

CHAPTER 14

WITH THE SECURITY-CLEARED MAJOR Cook acting as his chaperone, Morgan decided it was time to take a look at where the kidnapper had threatened to play his endgame.

'Security's impressive,' he assessed as they cleared their second checkpoint, this one taking them from Birdcage Walk to Horse Guards Road and along the eastern edge of St James's Park, now cloaked in darkness.

'They'll start ramping it up in the morning,' Cook assured him. 'By the time the crowds begin to turn up, there'll be police and military all over the streets.'

'And in the buildings,' Morgan was certain. 'There'll be a few bored snipers eyeballing us right now.'

The pair walked on in silence, both searching for vulnerable points around the parade ground.

There were many.

'What's to stop someone coming in from the War Rooms on the southern side?' Morgan asked. 'The public have access to that. Could someone hide out in there?'

'It's closed the day of the Trooping,' Cook explained, 'and it was searched with dogs last night. The same will happen again this morning.'

'What about this park? That's a long border to cover.'

'Foot patrols, static guards, CCTV and drones.'

'That should do it.'

'It should,' Cook agreed.

The pair came to the parade ground itself. Tiers of seating and bleachers were arranged for the spectators that would flank the royal dais. On the gravel stood the small markers that signified the placement of each of the parading company's troops.

Morgan turned to Cook, planning to ask her about the bleachers, but he held his tongue. Her eyes were on a memorial across the road that was bathed in light, the stone column lined with the figures of pensive soldiers in the uniform of the trenches.

'The Guards Division Memorial,' she told him, sombre.

'Someone you knew?' Morgan guessed.

'John. A good friend of mine. He was killed in Babaji, Afghanistan.'

'I'm sorry,' he offered.

'I know you are.' She smiled weakly. 'Your background is no secret, Jack. I know you get it.'

There was no reply Morgan could give. Like all veterans of combat, he did get it. 'It' was an unspoken shared experience, good and bad.

'I have a question,' she said suddenly.

Morgan wondered whether it would be one about the past or the present. He prayed it would be the latter.

'Why are we here, Jack?' she asked with genuine confusion.

Morgan could see there was more, and a look let her know that it was OK to say it.

'Our job is to save Abbie, yes? If the kidnapper comes as far as the parade, then Abbie's head's already in a bag.'

'Agreed,' Morgan said simply.

'Then why are we here?'

'Because we're working backward. They can't kill her here, that's obvious, so they have to do it somewhere else. Clearing security takes time. We've been held up twice for fifteen minutes, and that's with no line and no crowds.'

'I see where you're going.' Cook nodded her head.

'Then run with it,' Morgan challenged softly.

'Everything about the parade's timing is precise, and made public. Our kidnapper wanted the head rolling in front of the cameras, and there's only one point in the parade where they can guarantee that – the march past the Queen.'

'Right,' he said, 'and they're going to need to be in position far ahead of time so that they don't draw attention. When you have a parade full of soldiers standing frozen, any movement catches your eye. If they have the background we think they do, they'll know that, and so they'll be in position far enough ahead of time to avoid drawing attention. They're going to need an escape route too. A way they can get out when everyone's eyes are the other way.'

'The march past is at noon,' Cook told him from memory.

'And the deadline for the ransom is at eleven. We figure out how long it will take to kill her and get in position here, then we have a radius for how close they must be.'

'Makes sense.'

'Sometimes you have to work these things from the tail end,' said Morgan.

Cook smiled. 'Sure.'

'What?'

'You know that even a small radius in central London is going to include literally thousands of properties, vehicles and boats, let alone people, don't you?'

This time it was Morgan's turn to grin. 'You didn't want to work for me because you thought it would be easy, did you?'

CHAPTER 15

THE SENTRY SALUTED MAJOR Jane Cook as she led Morgan clear of the security perimeter and towards Whitehall. Even at the late hour, gaggles of tourists mixed with the civil servants who emerged bleary-eyed from the magnificently appointed buildings that had once been the heart of the world's most powerful empire.

Cook caught Morgan's appraising eye on the many poppy wreaths and memorials that lined the route to the Ministry of Defence.

'Miss it?' she asked. Morgan didn't need to be told that she was asking after his own service.

'Every day,' he answered honestly. 'I loved my job, and I loved my people. I do now . . .'

'But it's different?'

'It is different.'

'Now you're the general,' Cook observed with a smile.

'A general is nothing without his troops.' Morgan brushed the compliment aside. 'And I have great troops. The best.'

'You were never tempted to re-enlist?'

He smiled. 'Getting cold feet about leaving?' he asked, not unkindly.

'Of course.' Cook shrugged. 'It's the only job I've ever known. I was sponsored through university, and at Sandhurst at twenty-one. The whole of my adult life I've worn the uniform, but times are changing. We can't afford more wars, and the public wouldn't back them even if we could.'

'You think you'll be bored if you stay on?'

'I know I would be. War is a terrible thing, of course, but it's what you train for. I had that off the bat, and I don't want to spend the next ten years overseeing exercises on tighter and tighter budgets while the real action goes on without us.'

'So you're a war junky?' Morgan teased.

'I'm a soldier, Jack, and I live for a challenge.' Cook smiled back, and Morgan's pulse quickened with the knowledge that *he* was a part of that thrill-seeking.

He opened his mouth to reply, Cook's pace slowing, expectantly, but Morgan's chance to speak was lost as his and Cook's mobile phones began to ring simultaneously.

'Go,' Morgan answered, having seen the number of Private London's HQ on his screen.

'It's another call coming into the Duke's line,' Hooligan informed them.

'Trace?'

'Blocked. Great encryption.'

'OK. Patch us in.'

Seconds later, the phone's speaker emitted the metallic rasp of the kidnapper's altered voice. 'How are you sleeping, Duke?' he seemed to cackle.

'How's my daughter?' Morgan heard the Duke plead.

'Well enough, but just to show you I'm not playing games, you'll find a present in the old furniture warehouse on Kingsmill Road.'

'Kingsmill Road?' the Duke repeated.

'Battersea,' the kidnapper said. 'And don't bother calling the filth. You can send your friends from Private along to collect it and clean this one up. You hear that, Mr Private Investigators? I'm sure you're listening. Looks like you've branched out into sanitation now.'

'What do you mean?' The Duke stumbled over his words. 'Private? I don't—'

'Shut the fuck up,' snapped the kidnapper's harsh voice. 'Next call will be the last, tomorrow at ten to arrange the drop. Out.'

The line clicked dead.

'We're clear from the Duke,' Hooligan informed the investigators.

'He said "out",' Cook observed. 'That's ingrained voice procedure. He has to be long-term military.'

'What did he mean by "don't bother calling the filth"?' Morgan asked the group, the American not recognising the slang.

'It means the police,' Knight answered. 'So what now?'

'Everyone meet at Kingsmill Road, but wait three hundred yards to the south. We go in together in case there are any surprises. Hooligan, bring your full set of forensics gear.'

'Will do, boss. What are you expecting to find?'

Morgan thought back to the pool of blood in Abbie's penthouse apartment.

'Our donor.'

CHAPTER 16

HAVING MET HOOLIGAN AND Knight's van on a quiet street in Battersea, Morgan's Range Rover led the Private convoy to the front of a fire-damaged furniture store.

'Riots,' Cook guessed, seeing Morgan inspecting the destruction. 'They're probably still waiting on the plans to redevelop it.' Cook stopped short of her next words.

'Go on,' Morgan encouraged.

'You think pulling up like this is the best idea?' she asked, as neutrally as she could.

'Don't ever be afraid to disagree with me, Jane.' He smiled. 'But I think we're good. Our guys could be ex-military, but I don't think they'll have RPGs.'

'True.' Cook nodded. 'But they probably do have a good knowledge of how to make use of IEDs. There's all kinds of rubbish and litter around here where they could hide one.'

'And what would they gain from that?' Morgan asked, interested.

'Time. They take out the people who're getting close to them, or why else do they put something out here for us as a distraction?

It's either desperation or a trap. If we're all dead, it doesn't matter to the kidnapper. The Duke's not with us, and he's the one paying the ransom.'

Morgan thought it over.

'Keep thinking like that,' he told her, pleased, then spoke into a small button radio affixed to the neck of his hoody. 'Knight, hold back here for now. I'm going to give the place a once-over. Take the van a hundred yards back.'

Knight's reply betrayed his unease with the order, but Morgan was his leader. 'If that's what you want,' the Brit answered, and the van reversed back along the street.

Scanning for wires that could lead to a firing point for any explosives, Morgan made his way cautiously to the front of the building. It had at one point been boarded up, but the chipboard was now ripped and torn, the graffiti dull.

He saw that there were several points of entry, which made him feel more at ease about an ambush. If he was setting a trap, the kidnapper would want to funnel the Private personnel into a chosen killing ground. It made no sense to allow them to clear the obstruction of the shopfront, only to try to ensnare them inside.

Pushing himself between the boards, Morgan eased into the shop and quickly moved five paces to his left, crouching into the deepest shadows. There he waited and listened for almost a minute. The only sounds were the Range Rover's idling engine and the scurrying of mice.

He turned on his flashlight. The beam cut through the darkness and played across the charred metal skeletons of beds and sofas.

He saw nothing that put his senses on edge, so he got to his feet and slowly edged his way into what had been a display room. The torchlight shone on empty beer cans, the stubs of cigarettes and the general debris of the homeless. None of it was fresh. There was no odour to it.

No odour to hide the smell that now hit Morgan like a fist.

He was very familiar with it.

It was the smell of death.

CHAPTER 17

MORGAN SPOKE INTO THE mic on his collar. 'Guys, come in through the front. Hooligan, bring all your tools. Peter?'

'Yes, Jack?'

'We have body bags in that van?'

'We do,' Knight answered. Morgan didn't need to tell him to bring one in.

Head-torch beams criss-crossing the furniture store as they walked, the trio came up beside Morgan, whose own Maglite beam was unflinching. Knight and the others followed its direction.

The torch lit up the face of a young woman. She was dead, and there was no elegance or dignity in her posture.

'I thought we were going to find Aaron Shaw,' Knight said. 'This must be the second hostage.'

'I know her,' Cook spoke up suddenly.

The three men turned to her in surprise.

'You do?' Knight asked.

'Her name's Grace Beckit. She's a society girl. She was a model, but mostly she was known for her partying.'

'She was also a close friend of Abbie's,' Knight confirmed after a quick Internet search on his phone.

Cook took a step closer to the body, her torchlight revealing a savage cut to Grace's throat.

'Christ. They butchered the poor girl.'

'A butcher would show more humanity,' Hooligan said, preparing his kit for sample-taking.

Cook noticed the preparations. She turned to Morgan, who was stony-faced and silent. 'I think it's time we called in the police, Jack. We kept them out to preserve life, but this girl's already gone. You're investigators, not a SWAT team, and I think this case is going to need both.'

Morgan thought for a moment.

'It's too late for Grace, Jane. Whatever happens next, Grace is gone, but as far as we know, Abbie is still alive. Keeping her that way is our priority, so we have to do as the kidnappers say and keep the police out of this.'

'Someone needs to answer for this,' Cook told him.

'And they will,' Morgan promised, his eyes ablaze in the darkness. 'This doesn't end when Abbie is safe, Jane. It ends when we find the bastard who did this, and he pays for what he's done.'

CHAPTER 18

PRIVATE HQ DID NOT possess a gurney, so Grace's covered body was carried into the building on a spinal board, Morgan and Knight acting as solemn pallbearers.

As they walked through reception, Sadie Wilkinson, Abbie's publicist – who had remained at Private awaiting Knight's return – saw the body bag.

'Abbie!' she cried out.

Cook caught her, the powerful soldier holding back the struggling woman.

'It's not Abbie,' Cook said soothingly. Wilkinson's wild eyes looked at her questioningly.

Knight recalled seeing in the briefing Private's intelligence section had put together on Abbie's publicist that she also represented Grace Beckit. He gestured that he and Morgan should lay their burden down, and then he stepped towards the woman in Cook's arms.

'It's not Abbie,' he told her. 'It's Grace.'

'No!' Wilkinson cried, her body shaking. 'No!'

Knight stepped across, and with his arms firmly around the woman's shoulders he took her from Cook's hold.

'I'll handle this,' he mouthed to Morgan, and led the woman away on her unsteady feet, the publicist near-paralysed from shock.

'Didn't look like there was any relief when she found out it wasn't Abbie,' Hooligan observed, and explained to Morgan and Cook that Wilkinson was the kidnapped girl's publicist.

'She's probably Grace's rep too,' Morgan guessed.

Having been directed there by Knight, two members of Private staff arrived and, with Hooligan, carried Grace's body to where it could be kept in the lab's cold storage facility.

Left alone with Cook, Morgan shook his head, unhappy at the turn of events.

'She shouldn't have had to see that.'

'It's not your fault,' Cook assured him. 'You couldn't have known.'

'I'm the head of Private, Jane. Everything that goes on in my company is ultimately on me.'

With another shake of his head, Morgan realised he was talking to a prospective future employee, and not just a beautiful woman who was impressing him with her guts and vision.

'You know what? It's done,' he said, regaining his composure. 'We need to concentrate on Abbie. I'm going to call Flex, see if he's come up with anything.'

'I'll go get us some coffee.'

Left alone for the first time since the afternoon, Morgan took a few moments to clear his head. He took deep breaths and thought about the view from his home, the Pacific Ocean waves crashing over the rocks. Feeling centred, he dialled the number for Flex's office.

'All right, Jack?' the muscled man answered the phone.

'That depends on what you tell me,' Morgan said, trying to sound light-hearted.

'Then you're buggered, mate, I'm afraid. No luck with anyone I've talked to so far.'

'Someone must have employed Shaw,' Morgan urged. 'His last client was a private hire, as they served together, but there must be a trace of him elsewhere?'

'There are a few companies who keep regular office hours, so I haven't had a chance to call them. Could be they turn something up.'

'Great. Thanks, Flex.'

'No problem, mate. Anything else I can help you with, before I go get some gonk?'

'Gonk?'

'Ha, sorry, mate. Army term for sleep. Got a big gym session in the morning. Got to rest sometime.'

'Yeah, you could use some more time in the gym,' Morgan joked. 'Don't take this the wrong way, Flex, but I have to ask it . . .'

'Go on.'

'When you were making these calls, did you mention to anyone who was behind the questions?'

'Of course not, Jack. OPSEC, mate,' Flex answered, meaning operational security – a term common to both of the men's services.

'Thanks. I knew you wouldn't, but the kidnapper somehow found out Private are working this,' Morgan explained. 'There's a leak somewhere, so I had to ask. You know how it is.'

'That I do, mate,' Flex replied. 'I'll check in with you tomorrow.'

Morgan hadn't liked to ask a fellow security professional about a basic matter of information security – to a man of Flex's experience, it could have been taken as deeply insulting – but Morgan was looking forward to his next phone call even less.

'Your Grace?' he said. 'I hope I didn't wake you.'

'No,' the Duke answered, sounding as if he'd aged a further ten years since earlier that evening. 'No, Mr Morgan. Not while my daughter is still missing.'

'We'll get Abbie back to you safe, sir,' Morgan promised, thinking about the savage wound to Grace's throat.

'I only hope you can, Mr Morgan,' the Duke choked. 'Getting the money is not . . . I don't have that amount of money.'

This wasn't a surprise to Morgan. His operatives at the Duke's residence had been keeping him apprised of the situation. Morgan had also dispatched Private's experts in insurance and financial matters to aid the Duke in raising the money, though all the risk would be borne by the Duke's estate.

'I had an idea,' the Duke uttered cautiously.

'Go ahead, sir.'

'We could release the story to the media. People love Abbie. Surely they will come forward with donations to save her life?'

Morgan dismissed the idea at once and proceeded to tell the Duke a rainbows-and-fairy-tales reason why Abbie's story should be kept private. What he didn't tell the terrified father was that a media campaign would likely scare the kidnapper into cutting his losses, and Abbie's throat. With one, probably two deaths on his hands, the kidnapper was fully committed. If the Duke could not raise the ransom, then there were only two ways the abduction could end.

Morgan would find Abbie in time, or the kidnapper would cut off her head.

CHAPTER 19

SEEING GRACE BECKIT'S CORPSE had shocked Sadie Wilkinson to a point of near collapse for the second time that night. Having sat her down and brought her water, Knight had decided he should take the publicist home.

The drive to Wilkinson's house had been quiet at first, the woman withdrawn into herself, her eyes wide with shock. Then Knight had remembered the publicist's earlier comments about his exploits at the Olympic Games. Though a modest man, he was anxious to get her talking, and out of her own head.

'So you saw what happened at the Olympics?' he asked, and, slowly but surely, Wilkinson was pulled from her trance. By the time she opened the door to her stylishly decorated home, she was explaining in detail how she would have capitalised on Knight's moment in the spotlight.

'You really love your job,' he told her.

'I do,' she agreed, seeming to be pained by her answer.

'I'll make some tea,' he offered. 'You don't mind, do you?'

Wilkinson shrugged and sat heavily on a sofa, her chin resting in the cradle of her hands.

'Grace is dead,' she stated simply.

'I'm sorry you had to see that,' said Knight.

'I'm not. I needed to.'

Knight wasn't sure what to say, but Wilkinson wasn't finished in any case.

'Life and death. It makes decisions easy, doesn't it?'

'I suppose it does. Or at least forces you to make decisions,' he said, not enjoying the conversation, but knowing he should let the woman talk out her thoughts.

He finished making the tea and moved to sit beside her, placing the cups on the glass table in front of them. With the keen eye of an investigator, Knight noticed the small grains of cocaine that Wilkinson had failed to clean from the table's surface.

'I don't want tea,' Wilkinson said after a moment of silence. 'Sorry, Peter.'

'That's OK,' he told her with a friendly smile. 'What can I get you?' He hoped she wasn't about to begin snorting lines in front of him.

'Nothing,' she said instead.

'Well, is there anything I can do for you?'

'Yes,' she answered, turning to face him. 'I want you to fuck me.'

Knight's eyes widened. Looking into Wilkinson's, he could see hers were ablaze – looking into death's face had filled her with lust. He sat immobile, so she made the decision for him, grabbing his head with both hands and pulling him towards her, pressing her lips against his and forcing them apart with her tongue.

'I can't,' Knight said, breaking away, his hands on her shoulders.

'Why?'

'It's unprofessional.'

Wilkinson stared at him. Looking into her eyes, he could see a woman caught between rage and sorrow.

'Fuck you, then,' she spat, before bursting into tears.

He held her and she sobbed into his chest. She cried for a long time, Knight soothing her. As a single father of two children, and head of Private London, it wasn't often that he enjoyed any kind of physical intimacy. Feeling Wilkinson pressed against him, Knight wondered if he needed the physical contact of another adult as much as she did.

She lifted her red eyes to meet his.

'I'm going to take a bath,' she said.

She got to her feet and left the room. Knight collected the cups of tea and threw their stone-cold contents into the sink. He felt terrible for the woman, whose relationship with Abbie and Grace obviously crossed the threshold from professional to friendship. With little idea of what else he could do to ease her suffering, he opened the kitchen's fridge – perhaps bathed and with a hot meal inside of her, Wilkinson could find some rest before sunrise.

Knight found a packet of chicken and the ingredients to make a stir fry. He looked around for a knife, but the long chopping blade was missing from the knife block. Assuming it must have been misplaced with the cutlery, he began to open drawers.

The first gave him nothing.

The second caused his brow to knit in surprise. Knight reached inside and took out a business card.

It was the card of Michael 'Flex' Gibbon.

CHAPTER 20

KNIGHT TURNED THE CARD over in his hands, wondering for what reason a publicist would need the contact details of a man whose security company ran mercenary operations into Africa and the Middle East. It was quite possible that there was an innocent explanation, but with Abbie's life in danger, Knight didn't have the time to wait for it.

He went to the bathroom.

'Sadie?' he called, knocking on the door. 'I need to talk to you about something.'

No reply came from within. Knight leaned closer, hearing the sound of running water. He looked again at the card in his hand, and then he remembered why he had found it.

The missing knife.

Knight let the card drop and reached for the door handle. It was locked.

He took a step back then rammed the door with his shoulder, stumbling across the threshold as the timber splintered around the lock.

Recovering his balance, he looked up and saw the blade beside Wilkinson.

But she was no threat to him.

She was no threat to anyone.

Sadie Wilkinson was dead.

CHAPTER 21

NOT SINCE THE DEATH of his beloved wife had the Duke of Aldershot felt so weary. The cancer that had taken his dear Elizabeth had been cruel and terrible, but at least he'd been able to comfort himself, however slightly, with the thought that it was a cruelty born of nature, and part of God's holy plan. What was happening to his daughter, however, was of a malicious bearing that he could never comprehend.

His thoughts turning inevitably to the ransom, the Duke looked at the sheaf of papers on his desk, left there by the specialists that Jack Morgan had dispatched from Private. The documents outlined strategies and detailed lenders who could possibly aid the Duke in raising the staggering ransom fee of £30 million.

Thirty million. Even if he could raise it, the Duke knew the legacy of his family would end with the payment to the kidnapper. All of the properties and estates, built by generations of noble blood, lost at a stroke. Lost because of his daughter.

She was not innocent in this, the Duke reminded himself. She had courted disaster. Invited it into her home. Abbie had every right to grieve for her mother, but she was a royal and had failed the test when it came to acting like one.

No, she was not innocent.

His bones aching from weariness and anxiety, the Duke crossed his mahogany-clad office, coming to stand in front of a framed photograph that held pride of place in the centre of the wall.

It had been taken twenty-six years ago, and the Duke studied the lines of soldiers who stood and kneeled in ranks, many sporting moustaches, the younger Duke's own nothing but a pathetic pencil line. It had been a dangerous time in Northern Ireland, and the Duke had revelled in the challenge. Standing beside him was Sergeant Aaron Shaw.

The Duke swallowed. Shaw had always been his man – solid, unflappable. It grieved him that his sergeant had survived the Troubles in Ireland, only to die protecting his daughter. The bond between officer and NCO could never have been described as friendship, but there was a deep-rooted respect and understanding born from comradeship. They had relied upon one another, and so, on learning of Shaw's very likely passing, the Duke had imagined that he would be saddened.

He wasn't. He was only angry. So many people had let him down.

The Duke moved to his desk, his sagging body almost disappearing into the depths of the high-backed chair as he sat. He was exhausted. He was finished.

Worse yet, his *family* was finished.

He heard a commotion in the corridor. He knew who it would be. He had expected him to arrive sooner and for the endgame to be played out, for the man's coming could only mean one thing – the Duke was doomed.

And so was his daughter.

CHAPTER 22

THE DUKE'S OFFICE DOOR opened so violently that it almost came off its hinges.

Morgan was the cause, his handsome face darkened with a snarl as he stormed in with Knight and Cook behind him.

The Duke's grey face showed no sign of alarm as Morgan slammed a piece of paper onto the mahogany desk.

'This is for you, *Your Grace*,' he growled.

The Duke looked from the note to Morgan. Then tears began to roll down his sallow cheeks.

'I don't want to read it,' he choked.

'Then I will,' Morgan declared and snatched up the paper. 'It's pretty concise, because Sadie Wilkinson was in a hurry to take her own life.'

A groan from the Duke confirmed that this had been his fear.

'That's right,' Morgan told him. 'Wilkinson is dead, and so is Grace Beckit. Now we know why.'

As the eyes of Knight and Cook burned into the Duke, Morgan went on to read Wilkinson's confession. Desperate to salvage Abbie's image in the public eye, the Duke and Wilkinson had dreamed up the idea of a staged kidnapping. It had been Wilkinson's suggestion that the young royal would have been released during the Trooping the Colour parade for maximum exposure, the contrast of a dishevelled and abused young woman against a strong and regimented military force a stroke of PR genius. Abbie had been ignorant of the plot, just as Wilkinson had been ignorant of the true danger of the stunt. She'd had no idea how Grace had become involved, but seeing her body had been too much for her. Wilkinson had not been able to live with the guilt.

'I couldn't do anything for her,' Knight growled, approaching the Duke. 'She was dead when I found her.'

'Three deaths,' Morgan spat, throwing the suicide note into the Duke's lap, then leaning across the desk so that his own face was in the older man's. 'Why?' he roared.

'They've gone rogue,' the Duke whined, tears still falling.

It was too much for the soldier Cook, who stepped up and drilled her fist into the ex-military man's jaw.

'Hold yourself like a bloody soldier, you coward, and tell us what we need to know!'

The blow brought some composure back to the Duke. 'Shaw,' he said. 'Shaw was handling it.' A trickle of blood ran from the corner of his mouth.

'Shaw's dead,' Knight stated.

'He brought in someone else. Shaw must have lost control of him,' the Duke told them, confirming Morgan's suspicions that Shaw had been killed by someone he trusted.

'Who?' he asked.

'I don't know! I don't know! Shaw organised it all, and Sadie took care of the money!'

Morgan cursed, knowing that their two best leads to Abbie were now dead. Before he could press the Duke further, his phone began to vibrate in his pocket.

So too did the phones of Cook and Knight.

'Watch him,' Morgan instructed the pair, stepping away. 'Morgan,' he answered.

'Boss, it's Hooligan. I matched the isolated blood I found at the apartment with Grace. She was there at the time of the kidnap.'

'Is there more?' Morgan asked, hearing the excitement in Hooligan's voice and expecting that there was.

He was right.

'I inspected the wound to her throat, and I think I've come up with the kind of blade that was used to kill her. It would also be consistent with what I thought cut the strands of fibre I found in the blood.'

'A hunting knife?' Morgan asked.

'A very specific one,' Hooligan confirmed. 'It's called a KA-BAR. You know it?'

But Morgan didn't reply. Instead, he hung up the phone and left the room, needing to be alone, needing to breathe.

Because the kidnapper wasn't only a killer.

He was a United States Marine.

CHAPTER 23

'ARE YOU OK?' COOK asked as a stony-faced Morgan re-entered the Duke's office.

Morgan nodded and turned his hard eyes to the Duke.

'We don't have any powers to arrest or detain you, but I'm assuming that for your own protection you'd like to be escorted to Private headquarters.'

The Duke understood that he wasn't really being given a choice, and gave his stuttering consent.

'Take him to HQ, Peter,' Morgan instructed Knight. 'I want you to work with Hooligan there. See if you can come up with anything about a US Marine working as a bodyguard in London.'

'A US Marine?' Knight asked, knowing it was Morgan's former service.

The American gave him a curt nod in reply. 'He used a Marine blade. See who you can find, then cross-reference it against Aaron Shaw. See if they cross paths.'

'Will do,' Knight promised. 'Where will you be?'

'The gym,' Morgan told him, without a trace of a smile.

CHAPTER 24

FROM THE OUTSIDE, POWER House Gym looked like any other industrial unit in London. There were no signs to announce its presence, or gaudy banners promising discounts on joining fees. Power House was home to a hard-core fraternity of bodybuilders and membership was by invitation only, each member being given their own key to the building.

Luckily for Morgan and Cook, the June dawn was already warm and muggy and a dumb-bell propped open a fire escape to let in some air. Sounds of grunting and shouting emanated from within.

'There's a lot of testosterone in there,' Cook commented as they approached.

Morgan stayed silent. The information that their kidnapper – *murderer* – could be a former comrade had left stones in his stomach.

They walked through the open door and into an industrial space that was packed with racks of dumb-bells and heavy-duty exercise machines of every description. Dusty mirrors lined the walls, and an array of flags hung from the ceiling. Morgan saw the red banner of the United Stated Marine Corps amongst them, its globe-and-eagle insignia staring down at him.

'Flex,' Morgan called across the room.

The big man turned. He was topless. His body was thick with muscle and scars. Alongside him, Flex's gigantic training partner shot an ugly look at whoever was daring to interrupt their routine.

'Who the hell are you?' the training partner challenged, and Morgan's fist clenched at the sound.

The man was American.

Morgan said nothing as he strode over to Flex and his partner. On an early Saturday morning, they were the only two training at the exclusive lock-up.

'This is Jack Morgan,' Flex answered for him, his eyes narrowing under his meaty forehead. 'What are you doing here, Jack? I didn't see any calls from you.'

'No calls,' Morgan told him. 'I wanted to ask you this in person.'

'OK.' Flex shrugged, trying to be casual, but Morgan could see that the big man was tensing to spring. 'What do you want to know?'

The time for tiptoeing was over. Morgan went for the jugular.

'Where's Abbie?'

For a moment there was only silence. A split second later, Flex launched himself at Morgan like a missile, but Morgan had been expecting the attack and sidestepped the bull rush, drilling a fist into Flex's hard skull as he stumbled past.

Flex's American partner wasted no time and scooped a barbell from the gym floor, swinging it at Cook's head in the same movement. Like a limbo dancer Cook arched backwards, the metal whooshing through the air above her head. As the American fought to regain control of the weapon, Cook rolled away to her right, taking a bar of her own from a rack.

'You twat, Jack!' Flex spat at Morgan. 'Who the hell do you think you are, sticking your nose into my business? My world!' he roared, charging.

This time he caught hold of Morgan and the pair tumbled to the ground.

But Morgan had allowed himself to be caught, and now threw his legs up around Flex's thick back and pulled the man's head down towards his chest. Flex was caught in the jiu-jitsu move known as the triangle, but with his immense size and strength he was able to prevent Morgan from closing his windpipe and putting him to sleep.

Metres away, Cook ducked and danced to avoid the wild blows of Flex's training partner. The man's veins bulged like snakes beneath his skin, and Cook knew he could kill her with the power in his swings. She also knew that, with muscles that big, the man would tire quickly, so she ducked and danced, prodding the end of her own bar into his rock-hard stomach when she saw the chance.

'Tell me where she is!' Morgan hissed into Flex's ear, fighting for leverage, his legs slowly slipping from the man's sweaty torso.

Flex cursed, and doubled his efforts to break the hold. Morgan could see there was no way to finish the move, and holding Flex in position was rapidly sapping his own strength, so he let go. Flex's sudden release caused him to shoot backwards.

Flex was on his feet again quickly and came charging once more. Morgan let him come, then knelt, picking up a small weighted disc in his hand. As if he had all the time in the world, Morgan threw it side-handed, as though skimming a stone at the beach.

The weight plate hit Flex in the centre of his face, smashing his nose and sending him staggering like a drunkard. Morgan knew it would take more than a broken nose to stop the monster, so he rushed forwards to take advantage of the moment and delivered a series of furious blows. A low leg kick to Flex's shin connected with a crack and forced the man down onto his knees with a cry of agony.

Across the room, Flex's partner had slowed down, his massive muscles outstripping the capacity of his heart and lungs to deliver blood and oxygen to them. His huge chest billowed as he fought for breath, his swings increasingly wild and ragged.

'You bitch!' he wheezed at Cook.

She saw her chance and stepped into the man's reach, thrusting her bar into his jaw. He dropped as if a switch had been thrown.

Grasping at his knee in agony, and seeing his friend toppled like a demolished skyscraper, Flex knew the game was over.

'You've blown out my knee, you bastard,' he hissed at Morgan.

'I'll smash out your brains if you don't tell us what we need to know,' Morgan threatened. 'Is that him?' he asked, pointing at the unconscious American. 'Is that the Marine who took her?'

Flex shook his head.

'He's an Army Ranger. Go check his tattoos.'

Cook did. Faded Ranger insignia were inked onto both of the man's shoulders. 'It's not him,' she said.

'But you know who the Marine is, don't you?' Morgan pressed, putting his boot against Flex's destroyed knee.

Flex howled. He knew now that to hold out would only cause him further pain.

'His name's Alex Waldron. He was a Recon Marine.'

Morgan cursed. Recon Marines were the elite of the service, selected for their mental and physical toughness.

'If you'd told me this last night, two young women would still be alive.' Morgan glared at the big man.

'I couldn't tell you because he's a bloody nutcase. I didn't want any comebacks. The guy killed a bunch of civilians in Afghanistan, but they couldn't prove it, so they found a bullshit medical reason to discharge him.'

'And you took him on anyway?' Cook asked, disgusted.

'I hire out the right tools for the right jobs,' Flex answered. 'And he's the right kind when it comes to "no questions asked" work.'

'You knew Aaron Shaw, Abbie's bodyguard, didn't you?' Morgan pushed the big man, who nodded.

'He came to me with a woman called Wilkinson. They wanted putting in touch with someone who could help them stage a kidnap. I gave them Waldron.'

'Well, it's not staged any more, is it?' Morgan growled. 'Three people are dead, Flex, including the two who came to you. What does that tell you?'

'It tells me the fucker's gone mad,' Flex grunted. 'He could have made an easy fifty K. Instead, that lunatic bastard jarhead went off the deep end, and he's gonna take that girl with him.'

'You could pretend to give a shit,' Morgan snarled.

'Oh, come off it, Jack. Like people haven't died to make you richer,' Flex sneered.

The words hit home and stopped Morgan cold.

Cook stepped in. 'Where can we find them?'

Flex shrugged. A sharp kick to his knee helped him to open up.

'In between contracts, Waldron and some of the other operators work for a haulage firm called Jones Brothers. They're big on hiring veterans. Maybe you can find someone there who knows more.'

'Where is it?' she demanded, threatening to strike again.

'Newington,' he answered, shielding the ruined joint with his hands. 'It's the other side of Westminster Bridge from Big Ben.'

'And Horse Guards,' Morgan said, his eyes lighting up. 'That's where she is.'

CHAPTER 25

COOK GUNNED THE ENGINE, blaring the horn as she used the Range Rover's size to bully her way through the morning traffic. Above them, the muggy June skies loomed heavy and grey.

'I think it's going to rain,' Morgan assessed with a pilot's eye for the weather.

He was right. Not thirty seconds later the clouds opened.

'You know any shortcuts?' Morgan questioned Cook, cursing as others in the road braked and slowed as the rain bounced from the tarmac.

'Nothing legal,' she replied. Outside, the rain ceased as if a tap had been turned.

'We can't risk the police stopping us.' Morgan shook his head, frustrated. 'Did you get hurt back there?'

'He didn't land a finger on me,' the soldier said, with more than a little pride. 'He needs to take some time off the weights and work on his cardio.'

'The beating you put on him, he's going to be taking time off from everything.'

Cook's smile dropped a little.

'I was praying he was our guy,' she said.

'Me too.'

'I would have beat Abbie's location out of him if he was,' Cook promised.

'I know.' Morgan considered giving his prospective employee a pep talk on the need for good conduct and rules of engagement, but he held his tongue. The truth was, Jack himself would have done whatever it took to get the information that could save Abbie Winchester – there was an innocent life at stake.

'Flex will come back at you,' she warned.

Morgan nodded. 'He will.'

'Ex-SAS and he runs mercenaries. The guy has a reputation to protect, Jack. You need to watch him.'

'I will,' Morgan promised, hearing the concern underlying the professional warning. 'Thanks,' he told her.

'For what?' Cook asked, taking her eyes off the road and meeting his.

'For everything so far, and for having my back.'

'Oh,' she said, and paused, weighing up her next words. 'It's a nice back to have.' Cook smiled, and the pair laughed. It was a laugh of relief as adrenaline wore away from tired muscles.

'We're almost there,' Morgan said, checking the GPS, then turning his serious eyes onto Cook. 'You're our liaison here, Jane. You don't have to come in for this.'

'You think Abbie's going to be there?' she asked.

Morgan nodded.

Cook said nothing more. She didn't need to.

Up ahead was the truck yard. The soldier brought the Range Rover to a stop and, with a look to Morgan, stepped out.

CHAPTER 26

MORGAN'S FEET SPLASHED DOWN into a puddle as he stepped down from the Range Rover, his eyes on the haulage firm's yard in the near distance. Leaving Cook behind, he made off at a casual walking pace, covering all four sides of the truck yard's perimeter. There was little for him to see save a line of trucks, a Portakabin office and rain-filled wheel ruts.

As Morgan had expected, Jones Brothers Haulage were closed for the weekend, the gate bolted shut.

'We'll go through the fence,' he told Cook, rejoining her at the Range Rover.

'You found a way in?'

'We'll make one,' he said, lifting a pair of bolt cutters from the boot.

'They could have CCTV,' Cook warned.

'If the police come, we'll either be gone or have Abbie. Here.' Morgan handed over the cutters. 'They'll be armed. This is the best we can do.'

'I hate doing this kind of thing without a firearm,' Cook confessed. 'I feel naked.'

'Come work for me in LA, and you won't have to be.' Morgan spoke without thinking, and Cook couldn't help a sly smile.

'But it's an option, right?' she said.

For the first time in hours, a ghost of Morgan's usual happy, handsome face appeared. 'Come on,' he said, trying to fight it. 'Let's go and get her.'

'We're not waiting for help?'

'You're in the artillery, right?' he said. He moved off, Cook following on his shoulder. 'When you're sending forward observers behind enemy lines to spot your targets, do you send the entire unit, or a small team?'

'A small team,' she conceded. 'And they call in the heavy stuff.'

'There you go.' Morgan smiled.

'OK. But who are our big guns?'

'SCO19,' he answered – the Metropolitan Police's firearms unit. 'If we find Abbie, and there's no way we can safely pull her out of there, then we'll call them in.'

Carrying the wheel brace from the breakdown kit, Morgan led Cook to a stretch of fence that was hidden from the haulage yard's Portakabin by a line of wheeled bins. Cutting a hole through took moments, then the pair ran low across the open ground to the cabin. The curtains were open. Morgan took a cautious glance through the window. The cabin was empty.

'We'll check the trucks,' he whispered.

The company's lorries were arranged in a single row, a mixture of flat-panel and dump trucks. Morgan and Cook made their way slowly around the dozen vehicles, looking into the cabs and listening for any trace of sound.

'Jack,' Cook whispered. 'Over here.'

Morgan came to her side and found himself looking at a truck-sized space between two other vehicles. It was the only one missing from the neatly arranged line.

'The ground's dry,' he declared, looking up to the sky and thinking of the recent shower. 'We just missed them. Damn it!'

'You don't know that,' Cook said, trying to be positive, but Morgan pointed to a rusty-coloured patch at the edge of the dry ground.

'That's blood. Probably Grace's blood. They held Abbie in a truck here, and now they're moving closer to the parade.'

Cook tried, but could find no flaw in the logic.

'It's nine forty,' she told him, looking at her watch. 'Twenty minutes until they call to arrange the drop. Will the Duke have the money?'

Morgan shook his head. 'He was never supposed to pay, but Waldron heard "Duke" and thought "billionaire".'

'So what now?'

Morgan's eyes narrowed. 'We've got an hour to find that truck, or Abbie dies.'

CHAPTER 27

IN THE LAB OF Private HQ, Hooligan turned in his chair to watch Knight pacing the room like a caged animal. 'You want to be out there, mate,' he stated to his friend and superior.

Knight shrugged. Of course he did, but he also knew that the Duke was their only tangible link to Abbie and her kidnapper, and Morgan had wanted him to be on hand to handle the next and final ransom call that was expected in nineteen minutes' time. Knight was also the head of Private London, and sometimes – as much as he hated to admit it to himself – that meant delegating the tasks on the ground to others.

He told Hooligan as much.

'Bollocks.' The Londoner laughed, his tone quickly becoming serious as he saw the incoming call from Jack Morgan. 'Go ahead, boss,' Hooligan told him, patching Morgan through the lab's speakers. 'Peter's with me.'

'Peter,' Morgan said, the Range Rover's revving engine audible in the background, 'he's been holding Abbie in a flat-panel truck. The company is Jones Brothers, but he's probably pulled off the decals or painted over them. I think he's moving Abbie closer to Horse Guards before he makes the last call.'

'Where are you?' Knight asked.

Hooligan pulled up a GPS tracking screen to show him as Morgan answered.

'Heading for Westminster Bridge,' said Morgan, 'but the traffic is packed. We need the police's help on this now, Peter. But low-key. Can you make the call to Elaine?'

'I can.'

'Put out a description of the van. See if we can get a location, but no intervention.'

'You've got it,' said Knight.

'Check back in with me after you talk to her,' Morgan told him and hung up.

'I've got an idea,' Hooligan said over his shoulder before realising he was talking to an empty space.

'I've got my own plan,' Knight said, running through the door.

CHAPTER 28

DESPITE HIS MONIKER – GIVEN to him as a rowdy teenager by his siblings – Jeremy 'Hooligan' Crawford, a few speeding tickets notwithstanding, rarely broke the law.

'I'm a bloody model citizen,' he said firmly, as if trying to convince himself.

He had grounds to believe the statement. After all, Jeremy Crawford had shown that, no matter what circumstances a person was born into, they could rise high with a dash of natural talent and a bucketful of hard work.

Hooligan had earned degrees in both mathematics and biology from Cambridge University by the age of nineteen. By twenty, he'd added a masters in criminal and forensic science from Staffordshire University. There he'd been headhunted by MI5. Hooligan had worked in the government's domestic intelligence agency for eight years before Private had lured him away with a staggering pay rise. In those eight years the East Ender had played a key role in building the systems that monitored London's surveillance grid for signs of terrorism, and as one of its architects, he knew of the system's weak points, its windows and its doors.

'I must be bloody mad,' he giggled nervously under his breath. Because he was about to break into one of those weak points.

CHAPTER 29

INSPECTOR ELAINE POTTERSFIELD WAS a long-term servant of the Met, the service giving her a salty edge that had led to her blaming Peter Knight for the death of her beloved sister – Knight's adored wife. It had taken the events of the London Olympics to reconcile the pair, and now Elaine was the doting aunt to Knight's two children that he'd always wanted her to be. Early on a Saturday morning, she expected that her brother-in-law's phone call would be an invitation to lunch, or perhaps to join him and the children in the park.

It wasn't.

'We're in the shit,' Knight told her over the phone whilst running at speed through the corridors of Private HQ.

'Let's hear it,' Elaine said, switching from loving aunt to ice-cold detective in the blink of an eye.

'There's a flat-panel truck around Westminster with precious cargo. Either Jones Brothers signage or freshly painted over. We need it found.'

'That's not much to go on.'

'I know,' said Knight. 'And we've got less than an hour to find it.'

'Bloody hell, Peter! If you want me to work miracles, I need a little more information.'

'You can narrow the radius down to one mile around Horse Guards.'

'Horse Guards?' Elaine asked. 'Today's Trooping the Colour. If there are lives at stake here, Peter, then you need to come clean – like right bloody now.'

'One life,' Knight confessed. 'And if I thought a full blues-and-twos response was the best way to keep them alive, then you know that's what I'd do, Elaine.'

There was a pause as his sister-in-law thought it over.

'I'll put out a call. Find and follow, no intervention.'

'Thank you,' Knight said and hung up the phone. He came to a halt at a desk to the rear of Private HQ's large offices.

'Can I help you, Mr Knight?' the motor pool attendant asked.

'Get me a bike,' Knight told him. 'A fast one.'

CHAPTER 30

HOOLIGAN'S FINGER HOVERED OVER the speed dial. With a wry smile he realised that what he was about to do could possibly spell the end of his career.

He pushed the button.

'Boss?' he asked as the call connected.

'Go ahead,' Morgan answered, his voice thick with frustration.

'I'm gonna give you bad news, bad news, good news, good news.'

'Spit it out, Hooligan.'

'Bad news number one is that Peter has left the building.'

'What? Where's he gone?'

'More bad news first, boss.'

'Jesus. Just tell me, Hooligan.'

'I may have hacked into the security service's CCTV network.' Hooligan held his breath, as Morgan let out his.

'You know that's a terrorism charge if they catch you?' said Morgan.

'I know. And I take full responsibility, boss, but there's a girl's life at stake.'

'You're a good guy, Hooligan.'

'I'm a great guy, boss. And now the good news – I think I've got the van. Flat-panel truck that's had a fresh paint job. Really fresh, like Daz whites. It's on Horseferry Road, about a kilometre south of Horse Guards.'

'They must have taken the next bridge to the south.' Morgan swore, and Hooligan thought he could hear the sound of the dashboard being hit in frustration. 'We're never going to make it through this traffic in time to cut him off, by vehicle or on foot.'

'Well, that's where the second bit of good news comes in, boss.'

'Hooligan, you're doing a great job, but please, just get it out.'

'Sorry.' Hooligan cleared his throat. 'It's Peter, boss. He's on a bike, and he's cutting through traffic.'

'Can he get to Abbie?' Morgan asked, suddenly more optimistic.

'He can,' Hooligan confirmed, checking his screens. 'He's going to intercept in one minute.'

CHAPTER 31

AS A MARRIED MAN Knight had been forbidden by his wife from owning a motorcycle, despite the amount of time it would have taken off his daily commute. In the years following her passing, he had taken up riding as a way to escape London, and to empty his mind of every painful thought as he concentrated solely on the road ahead.

He was in that zone now, weaving and cutting through traffic, the bike's 850cc engine roaring as he opened up the throttle and pushed through the crawling vehicles.

Knight glanced at the GPS strapped to the bike's handle. It showed two dots controlled from Private HQ by Hooligan. One was the position of the truck that was assumed to be the kidnapper's. Another showed Knight's own location. As he turned onto Horseferry Road, the two dots became one.

'I see him.' Knight spoke into the mic in his helmet. 'I'm going in closer.'

'Peter,' Morgan's voice came through the speakers in the helmet. 'Just stay on his ass.'

'How far are you guys from me?'

'Too far. At least five minutes.' He heard Cook curse.

'Then I'm getting tight on him,' said Knight. 'If he goes off script and makes a move, I need to be in place to stop it.'

'Roger that,' Morgan answered, realising there was no other option, but hating it nonetheless.

Knight eased his way around the final few cars and positioned himself in the blind spot for the truck's mirrors, seeing that the rear shutter-type door had been secured by a thick, shiny new padlock.

'Brand-new lock on the truck's door,' he told those listening in to his radio. 'I need to take a look at the sides and confirm this is our guy. Maybe the paint got washed out by the showers.'

Knight edged his bike out to the side of the truck and saw that his hunch was correct – the black of the Jones Brothers lettering was showing faintly beneath the fresh coat of white.

'This is our guy!' he said excitedly.

But their guy was a Recon Marine before he was a kidnapper, and as such, Alex Waldron knew something about being scouted as a target. The black bike and its rider had aroused his suspicion, and now Knight saw a thick-jawed brute staring death at him in the wing mirror. He'd been spotted.

And that was when Waldron tried to kill him.

CHAPTER 32

WALDRON HIT A HARD left and a right on the wheel, causing the truck's rear end to shoot out, hoping to send Knight and his bike smashing into the line of cars parked nose to tail at the roadside.

Knight saw the truck's movement just in time, and with a flick of the throttle the bike's powerful engine pushed him forward and out of danger. He was now level with the cab. Waldron threw caution to the wind and began to drag the corner of the cab along the line of stationary vehicles. Knight would either be ground between the truck and the cars, or if he hit the brakes and dropped back, another flick of the wheel would send the truck's rear end slamming into him.

He had less than a second to make a decision that would either save or end his life.

He took it, and with adrenaline pumping through his veins, he made the impossible leap to the rear of the truck's cab. The bike fell to the tarmac and smashed to pieces under the truck's wheels.

Somehow, amidst the chaos and destruction, Knight found a handhold, gripping on by his fingertips.

It was enough. Acting purely on impulse and instinct, he hauled himself to safety in the narrow refuge between the cab and its cargo container.

With a soldier's sixth sense, Waldron had seen the narrow escape of his prey and began to throw the truck into a series of wild manoeuvres in an attempt to shake Knight loose, the blare of horns echoing as other drivers sought to avoid the menace that barged through the London streets.

Knight knew he had to act before the inevitable happened and someone was killed by this rampaging truck.

He pulled the helmet from his head, grasping it in one hand, and used his other to pivot himself outwards so that the Kevlar crashed against the driver's window, cracking it. Through the spider's web of glass, Knight saw a look of pure animal rage on the face of a man who seemed to hold no value for life.

Knight swung again, and this time the glass smashed. Waldron threw a savage punch through the now open window that connected with Knight's jaw. The blow struck like a hammer, and Knight's feet slipped beneath him on the narrow perch of the door ledge.

Inches away from becoming a bloody smear on the roadside, Knight managed to regain his footing. He grabbed hold of the driver and the two men grappled, Waldron oblivious to the pedestrians and motorists who fled in panic from the weaving truck. Grasping wildly, Knight felt his hand come into contact with the truck's steering wheel. Seeing a line of parked cars, the pavement clear of pedestrians, he turned it hard left with all of his strength.

The truck slewed. Metal screamed as the cab ploughed into a lamp post that bent like a broken toothpick, the echo of the crash ringing out across the streets.

It all happened in a split second, and in that moment Peter Knight was thrown through the air like a rag doll.

CHAPTER 33

KNIGHT WASN'T IN THE air long enough to register the sensation of flight. One moment he had been fighting with Waldron through the truck's smashed cab window. The next, he was half inside the front windscreen of a Ford Focus, the shattered glass giving way beneath the force of his landing.

He wanted to lie there. The damage control centre of his mind was already telling him that he was bruised from head to toe, that his spine had suffered a blow, and that two of his fingers were likely broken. Looking at the awkward angle they'd assumed, he became sure of it. He wanted to lie there, but if he did, he knew he had about twenty more seconds to live – because Waldron was climbing from the truck's smashed cab, his face as bloody as it was angry, and in his hands there was a knife.

No, Knight corrected himself, it was a KA-BAR. It was the weapon that had killed Aaron Shaw, and had sawn open the throat of Grace Beckit. If Knight couldn't move, he'd be the next to be slaughtered.

Waldron was free of the cab and saw Knight, helpless. He grinned.

Ten seconds.

CHAPTER 34

WALDRON SMILED AS HE closed the gap. Knight had met his kind before – the sickest members of humanity who could only find pleasure in inflicting pain and suffering on others. In most instances, Knight was as fascinated by them as he was disgusted. On this occasion, seconds away from dying on the man's blade, his only thought was how to kill the Recon Marine first.

Waldron was on him now, his tobacco-stained teeth showing in a bloody grin. He could see that Knight was trapped in the Ford's window, maybe paralysed. With nowhere to run, Waldron wanted to take his time in dispatching his victim. It was only the panicked cries of onlookers that brought him back to reality. He'd have to make it swift, so he brought the knife high, aiming to plunge the blade into Knight's rapidly beating heart. Waldron knew it was over – but he didn't see Knight's left hand, or what it had grasped from the car's cluttered centre console.

Knight's arm shot out from inside the car like a viper, ploughing a ballpoint pen into Waldron's neck. The big man staggered back and roared like an injured bull. It wasn't enough of a wound to kill his opponent, but as Waldron clutched at the pen and blood spilled over his fingers, Knight had precious moments to extract himself from the car window.

'Call the police!' he shouted at the frozen onlookers, some of whom were preoccupied with filming the incident. 'Call the police!' he shouted again as Waldron came for him, KA-BAR in hand.

Knight sidestepped the first thrust, his body singing out in agony at the sudden movement. Waldron was fast, even with the wound that had left his neck with a bright red scarf of blood. He thrust again and again, but somehow Knight was able to evade the blows, and his confidence began to soar. Perhaps, after all, he could survive long enough for the police to arrive.

It was only when his left hand touched a wall that he realised he'd been played. Waldron had herded him like a sheep.

'Dumb fuck,' the Recon Marine growled, enjoying Knight's shock and driving the blade forward.

This time there was no escaping it.

The knife ploughed into Knight's midsection. If it wasn't for the protection of his leather and Kevlar biker jacket it would have driven below his ribs and up into his lungs, but the protective material fought back enough that only an inch of metal penetrated his skin. He gasped in agony, but took the opportunity to deliver a swift headbutt, smashing the bridge of the American's nose.

Waldron stepped back in surprise, the blade pulling free. Knight followed up his attack, pouncing on Waldron and taking him down to the ground as the bigger man stumbled back on the uneven paving.

For the frightened onlookers, there was no way of seeing who was gaining the upper hand. It was a rapid exchange of punches and elbows – a gutter fight, the blade changing ownership several times as both men fought for life.

But only one of them stood. The other lay bleeding out on the pavement, the KA-BAR blade buried deep in his thigh, his face twisted in terror as he tried in vain to stop the flow.

Some bystanders screamed. Others ran. Some of the younger ones stayed and continued to film.

Through their lenses, they saw a man stagger towards a truck. There was a padlock key in his hand.

CHAPTER 35

THE AIR INSIDE THE Range Rover was thick, and it had little to do with the weather of a warm and muggy June morning.

'I hate this,' Morgan growled. 'Where the hell is Peter, Hooligan? How far from them are we now?'

'Three minutes.'

'And the police?'

'Maybe a minute behind you.'

Beside Morgan, Cook was silent, her hands tight on the wheel.

'What's up?' he asked her.

'The same as you,' she replied, not taking her eyes from the road.

'No,' Morgan insisted calmly. 'We've been on the back foot for a long time. It's only in the past few minutes you've started gripping the wheel like you're trying to choke it.'

Cook said nothing.

'Talk it out,' he pressed gently.

'Something has set me off,' she admitted. 'A trigger. I don't know what it is, but I feel like there's a piece of the puzzle right in front of my eyes.'

'You just need to take your mind off it. If you try and focus too hard on it, you'll never get it. Keep busy with something else. Here.' Morgan handed over a radio and headset. 'Monitor this channel.'

'What is it?'

'It's the police frequencies. The more open ones, anyway.'

Cook's mouth dropped open. 'The police, Jack! The police!'

'What about them?' he said.

'The kidnapper – he called them the filth! He called the police the filth!'

'So what?'

'So, you didn't know what that means!' she said. 'You didn't know what that means, because you're an American!'

'And so is Waldron,' Morgan said, his stomach turning sour as he came to the inevitable conclusion. 'Our kidnapper's not alone.'

CHAPTER 36

ABBIE THREW UP AGAIN.

She was on her hands and knees, vomit on her chin and in her hair. The comedown from her drug high had already kicked in when her world had begun to violently sway and screech, the contents of her toilet bucket sent spilling across the floor and over her bare feet. It had all been too much for Abbie's stomach. She had puked, crying with misery as she did so.

She had then been thrown forward like an empty dress, crashing into the hard metal wall, blood running from her nose, her bones aching. She had stayed there for a while, curled into a ball and content to moan in her misery, but then the bile had returned and she'd rolled onto her hands and knees as she gagged.

It was in this position that she saw one of the walls to her cell pulled away. Seeing blue skies replace the swirling patterns of black and white, Abbie wondered if she was still tripping after all.

The harsh sunlight that flooded into the room made her squint, and she turned her head away quickly, only vaguely aware of a silhouette that appeared in front of her.

It was the silhouette of a man. The way he leaned heavily to one side reminded her of the injured soldiers she had once visited in hospital.

'Abbie.' She heard her name. The word was spoken through pain. 'Abbie,' the voice said again. A man's voice.

'I'm Peter,' he told her, and she looked up.

She saw a face that was dirty with blood, but there was kindness beneath it. An open honesty. Abbie didn't know why, but she felt as if she should trust this man.

He put out his hand.

'I'm here to take you home.' He managed to smile, but Abbie didn't see it.

She was watching a second silhouette appearing next to Peter.

And then Peter fell down.

CHAPTER 37

'GOOD GOD,' COOK SAID softly, hitting the brakes hard as the traffic ground to a halt behind the mangled wreckage of Waldron's truck and Knight's smashed motorbike.

Morgan was already flying from the door.

'Hooligan, ETA on the police?' he shouted into the mic on his collar.

'Ninety seconds.'

'Jane! Stay behind the wheel!' Morgan shouted. 'We've got sixty seconds! We can't get caught up with the police!'

He quickly moved about the scene, seeing the rear door to the truck's cargo container open. A glance inside was all it took to confirm that it had been Abbie's prison. There was blood on the floor, Morgan saw, but not enough to be fatal.

He then looked inside the cab. There was a bag there, a military-style backpack. He grabbed it and slung it over his shoulder. Then he saw a crowd of people looking at the ground and taking photos on their phones.

He ran over to them, and there he saw the body. There was KA-BAR buried deep in the corpse's meaty thigh.

'Oi!' someone shouted out as Morgan bent to retrieve the knife. 'You can't do that. We called the police.'

Morgan pulled the blade free. It came loose with a wet sucking sound. All it took then was a look with the bloodied knife in his hand, and no one challenged him again.

He glanced at his watch – twenty seconds until the police arrived.

He frisked Waldron's body, coming away with nothing.

The Range Rover's horn blared.

'They're fifteen seconds away!' he heard Cook call.

Time was up. Taking the blade and the bag, Morgan sprinted to the Range Rover, throwing himself into the passenger seat as Cook jumped onto the accelerator pedal.

The car roared away, leaving the carnage of the scene to the arriving sirens of the Metropolitan Police.

CHAPTER 38

'SEE ANYONE FOLLOW US?' Morgan asked. Cook shook her head. 'OK. Pull over,' he instructed.

She took the Range Rover to the kerb.

'What about Knight?' she asked.

'We'll find him,' Morgan promised. He opened up the rucksack he'd taken from Waldron's truck and peered inside.

'What's in it?' she asked.

'A disposal kit,' he answered. 'Hacksaw. Plastic sheeting. A hammer.'

'Jesus.' Cook shook her head. 'You find anything on his body?'

'Nothing. No wallet. No ID.'

'Maybe the other kidnapper cleaned up. Took them with them.'

'Maybe,' Morgan allowed. 'But I didn't really expect to find anything. He was Recon. He'd know to go out into the field sterile.'

'That may be,' Cook thought aloud, 'but you don't get into Trooping the Colour without a ticket and ID.'

'I don't think he was going,' Morgan explained. 'The way he was dressed – scruffy jeans and a T-shirt – he would have drawn attention at the event.'

'Then why say that? Why make those threats about Abbie?'

'Misdirection. Trooping the Colour had been the Duke and Wilkinson's plan. They would have been able to get Abbie in and release her. But you and I saw how tight the security was to get in there. Why would real kidnappers risk it?'

'To prove a point?'

'This was about money, not politics.'

'God, you're right,' Cook realised, crestfallen. 'Then the other kidnapper could be taking Peter and Abbie anywhere. Our only hope is that Waldron's partner tries one more time to make the demand.'

'He won't.' Morgan shook his head. 'They were quick to kill before, just to prove a point. He won't have any second thoughts about doing it now to clean up. I mean they killed the bodyguard before they'd even . . .' He fell silent, his eyes growing wide.

'What?' Cook asked, looking at Morgan.

'We've been working on assumptions, Jane,' he told her. 'We assumed the threat to kill Abbie and make it public at the parade was real. That was wrong. What else have we assumed?'

Cook had no answer.

Morgan hit speed dial. 'Hooligan. Bring up the dead bodyguard's records.'

'Done,' came the Londoner's swift reply.

'Was he medically trained?' Morgan asked, his fingers tightly gripping the phone.

'Sergeant Aaron Shaw was a qualified team medic for every one of his operational tours, boss.'

Morgan looked to Cook, the scent of prey thick in his nostrils.

The Major almost gasped as she came to the same conclusion. 'Shaw knew how to draw blood,' she whispered.

Morgan nodded. 'Abbie was taken by her own bodyguard.'

CHAPTER 39

IT WAS THE PAIN beneath his ribs that brought Knight back to consciousness.

His eyes opened wide, and he wanted to scream in agony, but his lips wouldn't move and the sound died in his throat. It took him a moment to realise that his mouth had been taped shut. Wanting to tear it away, Knight discovered with panic that his hands were tied behind his back, his ankles also bound, and his shoes removed.

He was a prisoner, he realised, dread rising from his stomach. He had no idea how, but he had an idea by whom.

He was the prisoner of a ghost.

Aaron Shaw entered the room – the bodyguard whom Private had presumed dead was still very much alive. He was looking at a phone in his hand, as if weighing up a mighty decision.

'Will your dad pay?' the man asked, his tone heightened by adrenaline. Knight followed Shaw's gaze to another bound prisoner, though unlike him, Abbie Winchester had the comfort of a threadbare sofa.

'Abbie!' Shaw roared. 'Will your dad pay?'

Abbie's mouth was free from tape, but fear kept the words inside her.

'You useless little twat!' he screamed, brandishing a knife that he pulled from inside his coat. 'You still think you're bloody special, don't you? Even covered in your own piss and puke, you still think you're special! Well you're not!'

The man backhanded his prisoner, who let out a moan.

'Your dad was the same! Treated his blokes like they were his bloody servants! But who did he come to when he needed the dirty work doing? What kind of man would set up his own fucking *daughter* to go through this?'

'Don't you understand, you stupid little tart? Your dad would rather have you dead and out of the picture than give away the family's money! Why do you think he got these pricks from Private involved, instead of just paying up? He wanted them to push us into a corner! If he wasn't going to get what he wanted, then he wanted you dead!'

'No,' Abbie moaned, but the tone of grief in her voice led Knight to think that she believed it.

As if feeling the eyes on him, Shaw snapped his head around to face the man who had tried to stop him.

'You probably think I'm a sick bastard, don't you?' he said.

Knight was gagged, so he let his eyes speak for him.

'It wasn't me who came up with this plan!' Shaw shouted, slapping at his chest. 'It was her bloody dad! And it wasn't me who killed the girl! That was that prick Waldron. All I did was do as the Duke said, like when we were in the regiment, and now I'm the one left holding the bucket! I'm the one who's going to go to prison!'

He seemed to sag as he realised how compromised his situation was. In an instant he became calm. Almost remorseful.

'I've got no choice now,' he told Knight. 'I've got to cut my losses and extract. I'm sorry.'

Knight knew what the man's next words would be before he said them.

'I've got to kill you.'

CHAPTER 40

SHAW STALKED TOWARDS HIS bound prey.

Knight's eyes went wide as they fixed onto the blade in the man's hand, the hunting knife looming as large as a samurai sword. Despite the burning agony of his wounds, Knight tried to stand, desperate to fight no matter how doomed his cause.

Shaw saw his struggle and hissed, 'Stop moving! You want to go out in pain, or you want it quick? Just shut your eyes and I'll make it quick!'

But Knight had no desire to go quietly. The thought of never seeing his children again was enough to give him the energy to rock back onto his shoulders and propel himself forwards, his feet connecting with Shaw's chest.

'You stupid arsehole!' Shaw raged. 'For that, you can bleed out slow!' He took hold of Knight's struggling legs in one hand and prepared to drive home his blade with the other.

And then the window shattered.

CHAPTER 41

MORGAN PUT EVERY OUNCE of his strength into hurling the rubbish bin at the dirt-covered window. The metal smashed the single glazing with ease. Knowing that his moment of surprise would be measured in milliseconds, he was already throwing himself through the opening before the dust had settled, shards of glass tearing at his clothing and skin.

He hit the floor and went into a shoulder roll. He instantly took in the room at a glance, seeing Abbie bound but unharmed on an old sofa and Knight a moment away from death at the hands of the wild-eyed Shaw.

But Morgan wasn't the only trained killer in the room, and the disgraced bodyguard jumped away from Knight, knowing that this new threat must be dealt with immediately. Shaw was fast, and before Morgan could fully recover from his explosive entrance a powerful swing of Shaw's blade sliced across the flesh of his upper arm.

'Drop the knife!' Morgan ordered as he sidestepped a thrust. 'The police are on their way, Shaw! Don't make it worse for yourself!'

'Yank bastard!' the man spat, thrusting again. 'Let me past or I'll kill you!' he threatened.

'I'm not letting you leave,' Morgan warned.

'Then you're dead!' Shaw promised, and stabbed forwards again.

This time, as he stepped backwards to avoid the strike, Morgan pulled a blade from behind his back. Shaw eyed the KA-BAR knife, recognising it.

'I know Waldron killed Grace Beckit,' Morgan said, wanting to avoid further bloodshed. 'You're not a murderer, Shaw. You've seen what this blade can do. Don't make me use it on you.'

Shaw laughed at the threat. 'Come and try then, Yank!'

Morgan thrust forward with the blade, finding flesh and grazing Shaw's ribcage.

'Flesh wound!' Shaw beamed, rapidly losing his grip on reality. 'Flesh wound!' he laughed again, before launching a series of rapid thrusts at Morgan's face and neck. Morgan avoided them, but then Shaw let loose a brutal kick. The steel toecap of his boot connected with Morgan's ankle. 'Ha!' Shaw shouted in triumph, seeing his adversary stumble. Pressing home the attack, he aimed the blade at Morgan's neck.

Morgan raised his arm as a shield and howled in agony as the blade pierced flesh and scraped bone. The pain was almost unbearable, but he fought through it, knowing this was his moment. His only chance. Either he would end it now, or Shaw would work his blade free and kill him.

Teeth gritted, Morgan pushed his wounded arm upwards so that Shaw's blade dug deeper until it was trapped. Roaring a challenge against the pain, he thrust his own blade into the kidnapper's left ankle, and before Shaw could even scream, Morgan thrust it again into his right.

Hamstrung, the disgraced bodyguard collapsed wailing to the floor, leaving his blade embedded in Morgan's arm. Morgan sat back heavily, his vision narrowing, body singing in pain, but with both blades in his possession.

Fighting against the whiteness that threatened to overcome his sight, Morgan saw Shaw struggle to get to his feet, but the man was as helpless as a newborn foal. Eventually he realised it, and turned his pleading eyes to Morgan.

'I don't want to go to prison.'

Morgan said nothing.

'Please,' the man begged. 'Finish me. Just finish me.'

The sound of sirens began to echo through the smashed window.

'You had an honourable life,' Morgan managed, teeth gritted against the pain. 'You could have lived it. I'm not going to give you an easy way out, now that you know what you really are.'

'Just kill me!' Shaw screamed, bursting into tears.

Morgan's sympathy had run dry.

'You killed yourself.'

Footsteps pounded outside the window. Seconds later, the door splintered from its frame.

'Armed police!' the masked men called as they flooded into the room. Cook, having guided them to the hostages, came in with them.

Morgan dropped his blade to the floor and looked to the dirty, threadbare sofa.

He saw the young woman there, her eyes wide. He knew she would struggle to come to terms with what she had witnessed, and the ordeal she'd suffered, but Abbie Winchester was alive.

Knowing as much, Morgan finally let the pain overwhelm him, a sheet of white covering his sight as he slipped into unconsciousness.

EPILOGUE

THE COHORTS OF RED-COATED troops moved as if they were part of the same organism, gleaming black boots crunching into the gravel of Horse Guards Parade as the columns marched past the royal dais. The Queen and members of the royal family stood to take the salute.

The Duke of Aldershot was not among them. For now he was in the care of Private's London headquarters, a pair of police officers waiting on their orders to issue the arrest warrant as soon as the detectives were happy that they had a watertight case. According to Inspector Elaine Pottersfield, Aaron Shaw had already offered to testify against his former employer and co-conspirator in return for a lighter sentence.

'How did you know he was alive?' Knight asked. He was seated in a wheelchair, his wounds bandaged by paramedics. Beside him, Morgan sat in his own wheelchair and bore his own dressings. Cook had called the men a pair of 'stubborn, stupid bastards', but Morgan had been adamant that he would see the parade. Knight had refused to leave his friend's side, and so the two men had been wheeled onto the gravel of the parade ground, painkillers and the precision of the soldiers' drill distracting them from their wounds.

'We saw a lot of blood, and expected a body,' Morgan answered. 'But Aaron Shaw's corpse never materialised. It was only when Jane picked up on the kidnapper's slang that we knew there must be a second kidnapper, and if they displayed Grace's body as a lesson, then why wouldn't they have done the same with the bodyguard's, and put that message out from the get-go?'

Knight filled in the blanks. 'He probably built up the blood collection over weeks. The Duke said that Shaw was under the weather leading up to the incident. He'd have been weak from it all.'

'Which is why he needed Waldron to do the heavy lifting,' Morgan agreed.

'He gave me a scare,' Knight admitted. 'Thought I was going to be gutted twice in one morning.'

'Hooligan says you owe him a crate of Carling.' Morgan smiled. 'It was him that found you. When I told him I thought Shaw was our second guy, Hooligan raided databases and search engines for any links Shaw had within a three-mile radius of where the truck crashed.'

'That was his place?' Knight asked, shocked.

'It was six months ago,' Cook explained, a hand on Morgan's shoulder. 'They condemned the building, and Shaw had to move out. But he kept a key.'

'He's a soldier.' Morgan shrugged. 'He wanted to know he had a fallback position.'

The trio lapsed into silence, watching as the final company of troops made their way by the Queen. Her Majesty retired to Buckingham Palace, awaiting the fly-past of the Royal Air Force.

When it arrived, Knight broke into a grin. 'This is my favourite bit,' he said.

First came the helicopters, their blades beating against the air. Morgan's stomach tightened as he remembered his own days at the stick, and the men and women he'd flown with. Then came the historic Lancaster bomber, flanked by a pair of purring Spitfires. Next it was the turn of the RAF's jets, the transports escorted by sleek-winged Typhoon fighters. Finally, the crowds gasped in awe as the Red Arrows flew over the parade ground in formation, trails of red, white and blue smoke billowing out behind them.

'That was impressive,' Morgan beamed.

'I'm glad you liked it,' came a familiar voice from behind them.

Morgan turned and saw the outstretched hand of Colonel De Villiers.

'I owe you an apology, Mr Morgan,' the Guards officer admitted with remorse. 'I'm sorry I doubted your talents. Rest assured that we will be re-examining Private's bids for other royal events.'

Morgan was surprised by the admission, but he suspected there was more behind it than gratitude for saving the life of Abbie Winchester.

'I appreciate that, Colonel, but right now our only interest in the royal family is the full recovery of Abbie.'

The Colonel smiled, his face seeming to strain with the effort. 'Ah, yes. About Miss Winchester,' he began. 'I'm sure you can appreciate, Mr Morgan, that affairs such as these are best handled behind closed doors. A scandal involving the Duke is to no one's benefit, and I'm sure that your discretion in the matter will go a long way in securing the very lucrative security contracts for royal events.'

Morgan held the Colonel's gaze. When the American spoke, the officer's stretched smile faded to a grimace. 'Abbie Winchester is the victim of a serious crime, Colonel, and it's down to her what action she wants to take against the people who committed that crime, including her own father.'

'I don't see that—'

'I'm not finished,' Morgan cut him off. 'Grace Beckit is dead, Colonel, and all of the evidence that Private has gathered has accompanied Aaron Shaw into custody. I expect the Duke will join him in the cells shortly. Scotland Yard will get the full cooperation of myself and my offices in their investigation, and those two young girls *will* get their justice.'

Without hiding his disgust, De Villiers turned on his heel and left as quickly as he'd appeared.

'You've made another enemy there,' Cook cautioned.

'But I've made a friend, too.' Morgan smiled at her. Beside him, Knight began to take a great interest in the parade programme in his hands.

'Maybe,' Cook allowed, tilting her head a little to the side. 'I do think I could work well beneath you.'

'It gets better,' Morgan promised.

'Does it?' she asked. Out of Knight's field of vision, the Major traced a fingernail along the back of Morgan's neck. 'So when do I find out how I did on my assessment?'

Morgan said nothing. Instead he looked up to where the smoke trails of the Red Arrows merged and blurred against the azure blue of the sky. Tomorrow he would be up there, on his way to a home halfway across the world, and the pressures that came with being the head of a global investigation agency. But tonight he would be a tourist.

He turned in his chair and smiled at the captivating woman in front of him.

'The parade was great,' he said.

Cook looked deep into his eyes. The slightest tremble appeared on her perfect lips as Morgan took her hand.

'Now show me what else London has to offer.'

ZOO was just the beginning...

STORIES AT THE SPEED OF LIFE

JAMES
PATTERSON
BOOKSHOTS

ZOO 2

WITH MAX DiLALLO

Read on for an extract

I'M RUNNING FOR MY LIFE.

At least I'm trying to.

My clunky rubber boots keep getting stuck in the fresh snowfall. Fifty-mile-per-hour Arctic winds lash my body like a palm tree in a hurricane. The subzero-weather hooded jumpsuit I'm wearing is more cumbersome than a suit of armor.

Mini-icicles crust my goggles. Not that I could see much through them, anyway. All around me is a wall of white, a vortex of icy gusts and swirling snow. I can't even make out my triple-gloved right hand in front of my face.

But that's because it's tucked into my front pocket, clutching a Glock 17 9mm pistol. My one and only hope of survival.

I keep moving—"stumbling" would be more accurate—as fast as I can. I don't know where the hell I'm going. I just know I have to get there fast. I know I can't stop.

If I do, the seven-hundred-pound female polar bear on my tail will catch me and devour me alive.

But, hey, that's life above the Arctic Circle for you. Never a dull moment. One second you're tossing a net into an icy stream, trying to catch a few fish to feed your family. The next, one of Earth's deadliest predators is trying to kill you.

I glance backward to try to see just how close the bear has gotten. I can't spot her at all, which is even more terrifying. With all the snow swirling around, her milky-white coat makes the perfect camouflage.

But I know the animal is near. I can just feel it.

Sure enough, seconds later, from behind me comes a mighty roar that echoes out across the tundra.

She's closer than I thought!

I push myself to move faster and tighten my grip around the freezing-cold Glock, wishing I had a larger gun. Do I empty my clip at the bear blindly and hope I get lucky? Stop, crouch, wait for her to get nearer, and aim for maximum effect?

Neither sounds promising. So I decide to do both.

Without slowing, I turn sideways and fire four times in her general direction.

Did I hit her? No clue. I'm sure I didn't scare her. Unlike most animals, typical polar bears never get spooked by loud noises. They live in the Arctic, after all. They hear thunderous sounds all the time: rumbling avalanches, shattering glaciers.

But there's nothing typical about this polar bear whatsoever. I didn't provoke her. I didn't wander into her territory. I didn't threaten her young.

None of that matters. She wants me dead.

The reason? HAC. Human-animal conflict. My theory that has helped explain why, for the past half-dozen years, animals everywhere have been waging an all-out war against humanity—and winning. It's why this abominable snow-bear picked up my scent from over a mile away and immediately started charging. I'm a human being and, like every other animal on the planet right now, she has an insatiable craving for human blood.

Another roar booms behind me, revealing the bear's position—even closer now.

I twist to fire off four more rounds. I pray I've hit her, but I don't count on it. With only nine bullets in my clip remaining, I start psyching myself up to turn around, kneel, and take aim.

Okay, Oz, I think. *You can do this. You can*—

I suddenly lose my footing and go tumbling face-first onto the icy ground. It's hard as concrete and jagged as a bed of nails. My gun—*shit!*—goes flying out of my hand and into a snowdrift.

I scramble on all fours and hunt for it desperately, feeling the permafrost beneath me start to tremble from the polar bear's galloping gait.

I could really use that gun right about now.

By the grace of God, I find it just in time. I spin around—right as the bear emerges from the white haze like a speeding train bursting out of a tunnel.

She rears up onto her hind legs, preparing to pounce. I fire four more shots. The first hits the side of her thick skull—but ricochets clean off. The next two miss her completely. The fourth lodges in her shoulder, which only makes her madder.

I shoot twice more, wildly, as I try to roll away, but the bear leaps and lands right on top of me. She chomps down on my snowsuit hood with her mighty jaws, missing my skull by millimeters. She jerks me around like a rag doll. With her razor-sharp claws, she slashes my left arm to shreds.

Pain surges through my limb as I twist and struggle, trying to break free with every ounce of strength I have. Images of Chloe and Eli, my wife and young son, flash through my mind. I can't leave them. I can't die. Not now. Not like this.

I'm still getting tossed around like crazy, but with all the strength I can muster, I shove the tip of my Glock against the bottom of the polar bear's chin, just inches from my own.

I fire my last three shots point-blank.

A mist of hot blood sprays my face as the bullets tear through the behemoth's brain. She stops moving instantly, as if she were a toy and I'd just flipped her off switch. Then all seven hundred pounds of her slump down next to me.

Seconds pass and I begin to catch my breath, relieved beyond belief. Slowly, with all my effort, I reach up and manage to pry my hood from the bear's locked jaw.

I stagger to my feet, instantly light-headed from the adrenaline crash. Or maybe it's the blood loss. My left arm is gushing from easily a dozen lacerations.

Removing the polar-bear-blood-soaked goggles from my face, I survey the massive animal that nearly took my life. Even dead she's a terrifying sight. *Unbelievable.*

I thought my family and I would be safe up here. That's the whole reason we're living in Greenland in the first place, to avoid the sheer hell of constant deadly animal attacks. So much for *that*.

I just have to remind myself: the rest of the world is even worse.

"YOU COULD HAVE DIED out there, Oz! What the hell were you thinking?"

My wife, Chloe Tousignant, paces the cramped quarters of our tiny galley kitchen, anxiously twisting the cuffs of her thick wool sweater, biting her bottom lip.

Chloe's furious with me, and I don't blame her. But I have to admit, I've forgotten how awfully sexy she looks when she's mad. Even scared or angry, my French-born wife is both the most beautiful and most brilliant woman I've ever met.

"Come on, how many times are you going to ask me that?"

This would be number six, for those of you keeping track at home.

The first was when I came stumbling back inside covered in blood—the polar bear's and my own. The second: when Chloe was helping me clean and dress my wounds. The third was when I went back outside again, the fourth when I returned dragging as much of the carcass as I could. The fifth was while she watched me butcher it. (I *think,* but I was focusing pretty intently on the YouTube video I was watching, via our spotty satellite internet connection: *How to Skin a Bear ~ A Guide for First-Time Hunters.*)

"I just don't understand!" she exclaims. "How could you—"

"Shh, keep your voice down," I say gently, gesturing to the tiny room right next to us, where our four-year-old son, Eli, is taking a nap.

Chloe frowns and switches to a harsh whisper. "How could you take such a risk? It was completely unnecessary! You know it's prime mating season all across the tundra. The animals are even crazier than normal. And we still have plenty of food left."

I take a moment to weigh my response.

The reality is, we *don't* have plenty of food left. We've been living in this abandoned Arctic weather station for nearly four months now. Originally settled at Thule Air Base, twenty-five miles away, with President Hardinson and a group of government officials, we had been on our own since they returned to the United States to manage the animal crisis more closely.

Chloe and I had decided to stay. We thought it would be safer. We hoped that living in such a harsh climate, home to fewer wild animals, would mean fewer wild animal *attacks*. And for the most part, it did. It also meant we were left to our own devices.

Yes, Chloe is right that it's prime mating season—because it's late "summer" and, relatively speaking, fairly temperate. But even colder, more brutal weather is just around the corner. Every day I don't go out there and trap a wild caribou or haul in some fresh fish to tide us over through winter threatens our survival.

As I stand over our little propane stove, stirring a gigantic pot of simmering polar bear stew, I decide to keep all of that to myself. Instead, I extend an olive branch.

"You're right, honey. It was pretty dumb of me. I'm sorry."

Chloe probably knows I'm just trying to play nice. A highly educated scientist, she's well aware of the Arctic's weather patterns. And I can guarantee that, as a deeply devoted mother, she's been keeping a worried eye on our rations. Still, she clearly appreciates my words.

"I'm just glad you brought that gun along," she says.

"Are you kidding? That thing's like American Express. I never leave my three-room Arctic hut without it."

Chloe laughs, grateful for a little comic relief. Which makes me feel happy, too. There's no better feeling in the world than being able to make her smile.

She comes up behind me and nuzzles my neck. I wince as she brushes against my bad arm, the bloody slash wounds throbbing beneath the bandages.

"Sorry," she says, backing off. "The pain must be awful."

It is. But Chloe's got enough on her mind. I don't want her worrying about me.

I turn around to face her. Her concern, her love, her beauty are all too much.

"Not too bad," I reply. "But maybe you can help me…forget about it for a while?"

She coyly arches an eyebrow. We start to kiss. Before long, things are heating up faster than the polar bear meat cooking behind me.

Until Chloe suddenly stops. She pulls away. "Wait. Oz, we can't."

I sigh, disappointed. But she's right. Stranded deep inside the Arctic Circle, there's not exactly a corner drugstore we can run to for some condoms or the Pill.

I simply nod and hug her. Tightly.

This isn't a world that either of us would risk bringing new life into.

"YUCK! DADDY, THIS IS GROSS!"

Eli has just taken his first bite of my latest culinary creation: oatmeal mixed with chunks of braised polar bear. He spits it back out into his bowl.

Chloe folds her arms. "Eli, where are your manners?"

How adorably French of her, I think. The world is falling apart and my wife is still concerned about etiquette.

"Oh, go easy on him," I say. "I know it's not exactly the breakfast of champions. But you do have to eat it, buddy. Sorry. We all do. Need the protein."

"No way," Eli says, shaking his head. He proceeds to shovel only the mushy oatmeal into his mouth, avoiding the meat. He uses his fingers, not his spoon.

I don't have the energy to put up a fight, and neither does Chloe. We consume the rest of our meal in silence. All we can hear is the eerie, howling wind outside, whipping against our weather station's aluminum walls. It sounds like something right out of a horror movie.

At least it's not an animal, trying to claw its way inside. It might be soon.

Chloe and I had come to the same chilling conclusion the night before. Because I lost so much blood out there on the ice, leaving a trail leading right to our front door, it's only a matter of time before *other* creatures pick up the scent and come after us. Like a charging herd of enraged musk oxen. Or a throng of feral foxes. Another polar bear, or an entire pack of them.

"All right, who's ready for story time?" Chloe asks, starting to clear our plates.

"Me, me!" Eli shouts, his face lighting up bright.

"Okay, then. Go wash your hands and get ready. I'll be in in a minute."

With a grin practically half the size of his face, Eli disappears into the other room.

When we first moved into the weather station, it was all so rushed and chaotic. Our main focus was making sure we had enough canned food and warm clothing. Toys, games, and books for Eli were the last things on our mind. Thankfully, we discovered the previous inhabitants were voracious readers. They'd left behind a giant library—everything from Charles Dickens to Philip K. Dick, though not exactly young children's literature. Still, Chloe and I have been reading selections to Eli every single day since. Most of the stuff is way over his head, but he loves it.

"Anything new in the world we left behind?" Chloe asks me, rinsing our plates.

She sees I've started skimming the *New York Times* homepage on my laptop. More than half the lead headlines are about the ongoing animal crisis, which shows no signs of slowing down. In fact, it's only getting worse.

I summarize some stories.

"Let's see. Researchers in Cameroon were testing a promising animal pheromone repellent spray when they were mauled by a horde of rhinos. President Hardinson just signed a controversial executive order to set controlled fires in federal parks to destroy thousands of acres of breeding grounds. And the Kremlin's denying it, but apparently a school of blue whales just sunk a Russian nuclear submarine in—"

"Enough!" Chloe snaps. She sighs deeply. She runs her hands through her auburn hair. I feel bad for adding to her stress, but she asked.

My laptop *pings* with a notification—a new email. But not just any message—this has been sent via a classified U.S. government server.

Its subject line reads: "Urgent Request."

I immediately slam my laptop shut.

"Now don't be ridiculous," Chloe says. She'd read the screen over my shoulder. "Open it, Oz. It must be important!"

"As far as I'm concerned," I say, "there are only two things in this crazy world that are important—and they're both inside this weather station with me. I'm done helping the feds, thank you very much. Remember what happened last time? How royally they screwed everything up with their so-called solutions? The idiotic bombing raids? The bungled electricity ban?"

Chloe puts her hands on her hips. Of course she remembers. We lived through every minute of that nightmare together.

But then she snatches my computer away.

"Fine. If you're not going to read it, I will."

She opens the laptop and clicks on the message. She begins to skim it, and I can see her eyes grow wide. Whatever she's reading is big. Very big.

"Let me guess. The Pentagon wants me to come back and try to help solve this thing again. But what's the point? They're not going to listen to me."

Chloe spins the screen around and shows me the email. I read it myself.

It was sent by a Dr. Evan Freitas, undersecretary for science and energy at the DOE. He explains that the powers that be in Washington have finally acknowledged that the animal crisis must be dealt with scientifically, *not* militarily. The Department of Energy is now overseeing America's response, not the Department of Defense. Dr. Freitas is spearheading the new response team personally, and he desperately wants me, Jackson Oz, renowned human-animal conflict expert, to return to the United States and join it.

"This is our chance," Chloe says, grabbing my shoulders, "to get out of this icy hell. To actually stop this thing this time. It's what we've been waiting for!"

I can see tears forming in the corners of my wife's big brown eyes. It's obvious how much this means to her. I'm still skeptical, but I know I can't refuse.

"You're right," I finally reply. "It is what we've been waiting for. It's hope."

A world-famous tennis player is stalked from Roland Garros to Wimbledon by a deadly killer intent on destroying more than just her career

STORIES AT THE SPEED OF LIFE

JAMES
PATTERSON
BOOKSHOTS

BREAK
POINT

WITH LEE STONE

Read on for an extract

THE MOSQUITO'S WINGS BEAT six hundred times per second as it slowly laboured across the hot clay. Accordingly, a ripple of tiny vibrations pulsed out through the thick afternoon air, buzzing and whining over the silent crowd. They had stopped shuffling. Stopped fanning themselves with newspapers and adjusting their oversized sunglasses. Stopped breathing, almost.

Because this was the moment of truth.

The afternoon sun beat down on Roland Garros Stadium and from the back row the two players were a mirage, blurred and swaying in the summer heat. They looked like old-fashioned gunslingers as they faced each other on the dirt.

The last two standing.

Kirsten Keller was twenty-three years old, and seconds away from becoming French Open Champion.

At the far end of the court, Marta Basilia was on the ropes. The world number one was a gnarly oak from Georgian farming stock. The old guard. They used to say she was unbeatable. These days, not so much. Plenty of pundits said she was heading for the inevitable downward slope that would only end when she became a pundit herself.

Meanwhile, Keller was an all-American superwoman. Young, supple, graceful and impossibly fast. The new breed. Basilia hated everything about her, from the blonde hair to the perfect bronzed skin, and the doe-eyed post-match interviews, and the impossible topspin she could whip through her forehand, and the squeals and grunts she exploded into every damn shot. And now she was winning. More and more. Audacious bitch.

The court clocks showed a gruelling two hours and seven minutes; neon-yellow measuring every minute of pain. Neither woman had given an inch. They were slick with sweat and blowing hard, but their steely eyes stayed cold. A lifetime of commitment weighed heavily on their backs. Their fans expected. So did their families. And their nations. And every losing gambler with a Twitter account and a nasty streak was lurking, just waiting to slay them if they lost.

Don't back down now.

The mosquito reached the far side of the court and came to rest on a fat man in the front row. The high-pitched hum stopped. The fat man forgot where he was and slapped hard at the insect, yelping as his hand connected with his own skin. A mushroom puff of nervous laughter bloomed across the crowd.

The umpire leaned forward in his chair and said, 'S'il vous plaît, messieurs-dames.'

The crowd settled, their eyes drawing back to the court and resting on Kirsten Keller's clinging white vest, slick tanned thighs and the bead of sweat rolling down the bridge of her nose. She bounced the ball twice just inside the chipped and smudged chalk line and blew out, long and hard, until she felt as calm as she could.

One more shot. Then it's all over.

She rocked back on her heels, a movement that began an unstoppable sequence. Muscle memory based on years of repeating the same complex series of movements she had practised since she was three years old.

She bent her knees, her right elbow heading backwards like an archer. Her left hand rose in one fluid movement, fingers stretching upwards as she released the ball towards the sky, simultaneously propelling her body forward so that her momentum would drive through the ball like a piston head. Her wrist twisted at the last millisecond to spin the ball and force it high past Basilia's outstretched racket, to thump hard on the cushioned tarpaulin at the far end of the court.

Except she never got that far, because as the ball left her hand a photographer clicked his camera and the noise of the shutter snapped across the silent court like a machine gun. Keller screamed. Not her usual ecstatic squeal, but a terrified primal noise that rang out around the stadium. She dropped her racket as if it were electrified and flung herself to the ground.

And then nobody did anything. The crowd stayed silent, with no idea how to react. Basilia eyed Keller suspiciously, wondering if this was some weird new mind-game. But it wasn't. After what seemed like for ever, Kirsten Keller got to her feet. She was covered in red dust from the court. Her eyes scanned the crowd wildly, she was gulping for air and she burst into tears. Then she put her head in her hands and ran from the court, disappearing into the locker rooms and never coming back.

THE PINK EARLY-MORNING SKY stretched out impatiently over London, testing the horizon, looking for weak spots. Chris Foster watched it from his office window. He had developed a reputation for being the best in the business, which made him a man in demand. Quiet moments like this were rare, so he let himself enjoy the calm. He watched the city pulling at the edges of the pastel clouds, and waited to see what the new day would bring.

Foster was sitting in a Knightsbridge office building that housed a bunch of high-end services: legal, medical, and his own offering of investigation and protection. It was the same job he used to do for the Metropolitan Police, only the pay was a million times better and so far he hadn't been shot or stabbed, or worse.

He sat behind an uncluttered glass-topped desk wearing an expensive charcoal suit and a fresh white shirt. No tie. Two buttons open at the neck. Same as every other day. Twenty-four hours of stubble, courtesy of a late job watching the back of an Indian steel magnate; but he wore good cologne and his dark-brown hair was cut short and tidy.

His assistant, Danny, walked through his open door with coffee and the morning papers. The three clocks on the wall between them ticked a little too loudly, chasing different time zones around the world.

The phone rang in the outer office and Danny headed back and picked it up by the third ring. The assistant's young face was unreadable and Foster smiled; he'd learned well, for when Danny had started he'd been too emotional and reactive. Now he took everything in his stride.

Without a word to the caller, Danny looked up at Foster. 'Tom Abbot?'

Foster instantly leaned forward. He hadn't heard that name for over three years, but it was a welcome surprise. Tom Abbot had always been a good man, and an even better officer. 'Yeah, Danny. Put him through.'

Foster tucked the receiver under his chin and turned his back on the seductive morning sky. Three years ago the two men had sat next to each other in a Metropolitan Police office with no windows and no sky. He almost felt embarrassed by his view these days.

'Abbot,' Foster said.

'Alright, Sarge?'

'There's definitely no need to call me Sarge,' Foster said. 'That was a long time ago.'

'Fair enough.'

'That's unless I need to pull rank at any point in the future, in which case you'll do as you're told.'

They both laughed, because it was an honest joke.

'How's your arm?' Abbot asked.

'Still attached.'

Under the tailored fit of Foster's suit, vicious scars traced the lines that the surgeons had cut in order to attach titanium plates to his radius and ulna, and his humerus and clavicle; which was lot of words for a lot of pain and the end of his police career. It was the end of something much more, too. It was the end of Elaina.

'I heard you left the Met,' Foster said, letting the unwelcome memories dissipate. 'So how can I help you?'

'I'm at the Paris embassy,' Abbot said. 'There's a girl who's been here for a few days. She's a tennis player.' Abbot paused. Inside the office the clocks ticked and Foster's eyes moved back to the window. Outside the pink-and-orange sky was turning a watery blue. 'Her name's Kirsten Keller.'

Foster, like 90 per cent of the world's population, recognised the name at once. 'The American? What's she doing at the British Embassy?'

'Using the facilities.'

'Using the facilities?' Foster asked. 'You make it sound like she's been taking the world's longest bathroom break.'

Abbot laughed. 'We've got a grass tennis court on the back lawn.'

'Of course you have,' Foster smiled.

'It's the only one in Paris,' Abbot continued. 'She's been training ahead of Wimbledon.'

On the line, Foster could hear the clicking of heels on a marble floor. High ceilings, by the sound of the echo. Abbot was on the move.

'We're hosting her as a favour to the US Ambassador,' Abbot said. 'She had a strange turn at the end of the French Open, and the press have been on her back ever since.'

'Okay,' Foster said.

'That's not the whole story, though.'

Of course it wasn't. Foster knew there were plenty of protection officers in Paris who could keep the press off Keller's back. There was something more, or else Abbot wouldn't be on the phone to him.

'Will you meet her?' Abbot said.

Kirsten Keller was Foster's usual type of client: professional, high-profile, rich. He glanced at his diary. His steel magnate was back on a plane to Mumbai and there was nothing that couldn't be moved. Besides, he was intrigued to know what Abbot was holding back.

'Sure, I'll meet her.'

'Can you come here? She's mid-training.'

'Sure,' Foster said. 'I'd like to see your tennis court.'

Tom Abbot laughed and then the line went dead.

JAMES PATTERSON

BOOK**SHOTS**

OUT THIS MONTH

Along Came a Spider killer Gary Soneji died years ago. But Alex Cross swears he sees Soneji gun down his partner. Is his greatest enemy back from the grave?

Humans are evolving into a savage new species that could save civilisation – or end it. *Zoo* was just the beginning.

Detective Harry Blue is determined to take down the serial killer who's abducted several women, but her mission leads to a shocking revelation.

A royal is kidnapped the day before the Trooping the Colour parade. Can Private's Jack Morgan save the day before kidnap turns to murder?

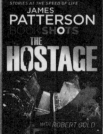

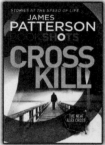

A world-famous tennis player is stalked from Roland Garros to Wimbledon by a deadly killer intent on destroying more than just her career.

Two rival crews attempt to steal millions of pounds' worth of diamonds at exactly the same time, leading to a thrilling high-speed chase across Europe.

When former SAS captain David Shelley goes looking for a missing friend, he enters into the same danger that may have got his friend killed.

A man is thrown from the top floor of a glamorous new London hotel. Can Head of Security John Roscoe find the killer before the bodies pile up?

JAMES PATTERSON
BOOK**SHOTS**
COMING SOON

AIRPORT: CODE RED

A major terrorist cell sets a devastating plan in motion.
Their target? One of the world's busiest airports.

THE TRIAL: A WOMEN'S MURDER CLUB THRILLER

An accused killer will do anything to disrupt his own trial, including
a courtroom shocker that Lindsay Boxer will never see coming.

LITTLE BLACK DRESS

Can a little black dress change everything? What begins
as one woman's fantasy is about to go too far.

LEARNING TO RIDE

City girl Madeline Harper never wanted to love a cowboy. But rodeo
king Tanner Callen might change her mind... and win her heart.

BOOK**SHOTS**

STORIES AT THE SPEED OF LIFE

www.bookshots.com

ALSO BY JAMES PATTERSON

Private Games (*with Mark Sullivan*)

Private: No. 1 Suspect (*with Maxine Paetro*)

Private Berlin (*with Mark Sullivan*)

Private Down Under (*with Michael White*)

Private L.A. (*with Mark Sullivan*)

Private India (*with Ashwin Sanghi*)

Private Vegas (*with Maxine Paetro*)

Private Sydney (*with Kathryn Fox*)

Private Paris (*with Mark Sullivan*)

NYPD RED SERIES

NYPD Red (*with Marshall Karp*)

NYPD Red 2 (*with Marshall Karp*)

NYPD Red 3 (*with Marshall Karp*)

NYPD Red 4 (*with Marshall Karp*)

STAND-ALONE THRILLERS

Sail (*with Howard Roughan*)

Swimsuit (*with Maxine Paetro*)

Don't Blink (*with Howard Roughan*)

Postcard Killers (*with Liza Marklund*)

Toys (*with Neil McMahon*)

Now You See Her (*with Michael Ledwidge*)

Kill Me If You Can (*with Marshall Karp*)

Guilty Wives (*with David Ellis*)

Zoo (*with Michael Ledwidge*)

Second Honeymoon (*with Howard Roughan*)

Mistress (*with David Ellis*)

Invisible (*with David Ellis*)

The Thomas Berryman Number

Truth or Die (*with Howard Roughan*)

Murder House (*with David Ellis*)

NON-FICTION

Torn Apart (*with Hal and Cory Friedman*)

The Murder of King Tut (*with Martin Dugard*)

ROMANCE

Sundays at Tiffany's (*with Gabrielle Charbonnet*)

The Christmas Wedding (*with Richard DiLallo*)

First Love (*with Emily Raymond*)

OTHER TITLES

Miracle at Augusta (*with Peter de Jonge*)